THE CASUAL DATE

A GRIPPING PSYCHOLOGICAL THRILLER

ALAN PETERSEN

17th Street Books

Copyright © 2025 by Alan Petersen

All rights reserved.

THE CASUAL DATE is a work of fiction. Names, characters, places, images, and incidents are products of the author's imagination or are used fictitiously. Any resemblance to actual persons, living or dead, events, or locales is entirely coincidental.

No part of this book may be reproduced in any form or by any electronic or mechanical means, including information storage and retrieval systems, without the author's written permission, except for the use of brief quotations in a book review.

For permissions beyond the scope of this notice, please send your request to:

contact@alanpetersen.com

JOIN ME

Want to be the first to get exclusive insights into my books, hear the latest news, and enjoy sneak peeks and more? Join my newsletter!

It's easy! Just sign up at www.alanpetersen.com/signup

Inspired By True Events

PROLOGUE

TRANSCRIPT OF GREENWOOD COUNTY 911 DISPATCH CALL

Date: March 7, 2024
Time: 8:57 P.M.
Dispatcher: Operator #329 (Olivia Cook)
[CALL BEGINS]
OPERATOR: 911, what's your emergency?
CALLER: (panting, voice trembling) I've–I've been shot! Oh my God, please...please help me!
OPERATOR: Ma'am, I need you to stay calm. What's your name?
CALLER: (choking, breaths uneven) Jade. Jade Sommer. I'm bleeding...please hurry!
OPERATOR: Okay, Jade. Where are you right now?
CALLER: Whitehall Park. By–by the Redwood Grove trail. (shaky breath) I was supposed to meet my boyfriend...
OPERATOR: Did your boyfriend shoot you?

CALLER: (sharp inhale, panicked) No! She—the bitch shot me!

OPERATOR: Do you know the name of the person that shot you?

CALLER: Hurry! I need help.

OPERATOR: Jade, help is on the way. Police and paramedics have been dispatched. Where exactly are you injured?

CALLER: (whimpering, breaths ragged) My side. I–I don't know how bad. It hurts...oh God, I'm going to die out here!

OPERATOR: Try to stay calm for me, Jade. Can you still see the shooter?

CALLER: (urgent whisper, frantic) I don't know—I ran. (rustling, quick footsteps over leaves). She might still be here. I have to hide...

OPERATOR: Stay on the line, Jade. Keep moving toward safety if you can. Can you get to the parking lot?

CALLER: (panting heavily, voice strained) I–I think I see it! It's close... (breathing labored).

OPERATOR: Good. Keep moving. Can you identify the shooter? Who shot you, Jade?

CALLER: (voice fading, breathless) I—

OPERATOR: Jade? Stay with me! Jade?

(distant rustling, muffled thud, silence)

OPERATOR: Jade, are you there? Can you hear me? Jade?

[CALL DISCONNECTED AT 9:01 P.M.]

ONE
ETHAN

ONE YEAR EARLIER

I WAS BORN and raised among the concrete and palm trees of Southern California. For most of my life, Los Angeles—the land of movie stars, sunshine and smog—was all I knew. It was home, for better or worse. Until today.

My Jeep Grand Cherokee was packed to the gills, as was the 6x12 cargo trailer I rented from U-Haul. I glanced in the rearview mirror as I drove north. The city stretched out behind me, partially buried beneath the hazy morning sun, a web of tangled glass towers, terracotta rooftops, and congested highways.

Like most Angelenos, I made it a habit to complain about how horrible it was to live in LA—the traffic, the crime, the never-ending cost of just existing there. But as I put more miles between myself and the city where I'd spent my whole life, I couldn't shake the feeling that I was making a big mistake.

Was I really cut out for country life? I'd always been an urban dweller through and through—a guy who found comfort in the city's white noise. The constant hum of engines, the blare of horns, a transient on the corner—off his meds, screaming at invisible demons—the distant wail of sirens. That was my normal.

Moving nearly 700 miles north to the backwoods of Northern California hadn't been my idea. But after the divorce, my ex-wife Kayla decided she was done with big city living. She wanted to go back to Fairdale, the small town near the Oregon border where she grew up.

Fairdale sat along the winding banks of the Trinity River, a rugged mountain town nestled deep in the heart of the Six Rivers National Forest. Surrounded by dense redwoods and towering peaks, it was part of Northern California's remote Trinity-Shasta-Cascade region, close to the Oregon border. Still technically the same state, but as far as I was concerned, moving there from Los Angeles felt like relocating to another planet.

Moving up there was fine for my ex. It was the magic of divorce—we were no longer tethered to each other's choices. She was free to do whatever she wanted, like uproot herself and our son to the boonies where she had grown up. But for me, it wasn't so simple. Tyler, our eleven-year-old, was still my responsibility; I wasn't about to be one of those part-time dads who only saw his kid on holidays. My father bailed when I was thirteen, and I'd seen him twice in the past twenty years. I refused to inflict that pain on my son because I knew it would affect him for the rest of his life.

I could have fought Kayla in court, could have made it messy and demanded that she stay in LA for shared custody. But the more I thought about it, the more I wondered if maybe she had the right idea. Maybe it would be better for Tyler to grow up breathing fresh air instead of the city's smog. Maybe being raised in a quiet town where people left their doors unlocked at night was better than learning to sleep through the sound of police helicopters.

In LA, an enormous chunk of Tyler's childhood would be spent stuck in the backseat, navigating the I-5, inhaling exhaust fumes. Our rental house was decent enough, but it sat so close to our neighbors that we could hear them sneeze. Owning property in the area was out of the question, unless we won the lottery.

Meanwhile, Kayla had inherited her grandfather's farmhouse in Fairdale—outright. No mortgage, no rent. A sprawling, two-story home on an acre of land, with the farmland leased to a local for extra income. Finally, she had a place that was truly hers.

A free house and a slower pace of life started to

sound better to me, so there I was on my way north to carve out a place of my own in Fairdale.

I was pleasantly surprised to find that there was a robust job market for IT professionals with companies in the forestry, agriculture, manufacturing, and healthcare industries. I landed a job before the move—desktop support specialist at a manufacturing company in Fairdale. It wasn't exactly thrilling work, but it paid well, had solid benefits, and came with a major bonus: the cost of living up here was a fraction of what it was in LA. So while my salary didn't jump much on paper, in reality... it kind of did.

Too bad we weren't moving up here as one family unit, but at least I would be close to Tyler.

I had plenty of time during the drive to think about my failed marriage. I regretted that I hadn't pushed harder to save it. Our divorce wasn't the product of cheating or explosive fights. There had been no fiery betrayal, no great scandal. We had simply drifted apart, two people coexisting under the same roof, rather than truly living as husband and wife.

She worked nights as a nurse; I worked days in IT.

We passed each other in the mornings and barely spoke before exhaustion sent one of us to bed. I don't know when it started happening, but somewhere along the way, we became roommates rather than partners. I should have seen it coming. But hindsight was pointless now. When she asked for a divorce, I agreed, although I didn't want it.

That was spilled milk under the bridge now. So the best thing for Tyler was for us to remain civil, and so far, we'd stuck to that.

A few months after Kayla and Tyler left for Fairdale, I followed. My friends teased me about it.

"Jesus, Ethan, take a hint," one of them had said. "Don't chase your ex up there."

They didn't believe me when I said it wasn't about Kayla—it was about Tyler. And if I was honest, a part of me didn't mind the fresh start either.

I had been to Fairdale before visiting Kayla's family. She had lost her mother to breast cancer as a teenager, but her father lived fifty miles away down on the coast, and her sister, Chloe, lived right in Fairdale.

The first time I visited, I was struck with how small the town was. I hadn't been here in years, so it still took me by surprise as I drove in. It was even smaller than I remembered.

My new place was a two-bedroom apartment in a complex right in the middle of town. It looked like it had been built in the sixties and was never updated. The faded sign out front read Redwood Apartments, but there were no redwood trees in sight, just a cracked asphalt parking lot and a few neglected shrubs. I started to regret having only toured it online, just like my job interviews had been over Zoom. But it was within my budget, and I'd only signed a one-year lease while I figured out if I could make it up here.

I pulled up next to the main entrance and ran into

the manager's office. He greeted me warmly and gave me my keys and a welcome packet.

Unlocking the door, I walked inside the apartment. It was clean, with a fresh coat of paint. Not bad. And unlike in LA, I could afford two bedrooms, so Tyler would have his own room when he stayed over.

Kayla would drop off Tyler in a few hours, so I got the show on the road and began unloading my stuff and moving it into my new apartment, cursing my decision to pick a second-floor unit.

I was tired and sore when Kayla and Tyler stopped by to check out my new place. I showed them around. Tyler walked through the living room and kitchen, which he could do in one take, then he took a quick glance at the bedrooms and wrinkled his nose.

"This place is kind of...small, Dad."

"Tyler. Be nice," Kayla said, gently scolding him.

Compared to our rental house in LA, and especially the farmhouse where he lived now with Kayla, he wasn't wrong. But I tried putting a positive spin on it.

"What are you talking about? You have your own room and your own bathroom." I grinned. "Champagne wishes and caviar dreams!" I said in my terrible Robin Leach accent, only to realize my eleven-year-old son had absolutely no clue who Robin Leach was. He stared blankly at me like I was the weirdest dad on the planet.

Tyler shrugged. "Yeah, I guess."

Kayla leaned against the doorway, trying unsuccessfully to suppress a grin.

Not exactly the enthusiastic reaction I'd hoped for.

It had only been ten months since the divorce was finalized. He was still adjusting. We all were. He still seemed angry at both of us for splitting up.

THE FIRST WEEK in town was a whirlwind that went by fast.

I started my new job a few days after moving in. The first day was nerve-wracking, but I settled in quickly. IT work was familiar territory for me—I'd been in the field for ten years. My coworkers were happy to have someone to fix their computer problems, and I enjoyed the work. That part of my life clicked into place rather smoothly.

Other things didn't go as smoothly, like meeting new people.

Making friends in a close-knit small town wasn't as easy as I thought it'd be. Most people here had known each other since childhood. They had tight circles of friends and didn't seem too keen on expanding it. They had family ties, a shared history. I was the newcomer from La-La Land Hollywood—though I corrected them, explaining I was from Los Angeles. I might as well be some rich celebrity type moving into their town.

Aside from after work happy hours now and then, I

had no social life. At first, I didn't mind. I was busy settling in, adjusting, spending as much time with Tyler as possible. But after a couple of months, the isolation gnawed at me.

In LA, I could go out any night of the week and find something to do. Here, it was different. Slower. Quieter. And lonely.

One night, after scrolling through old photos—pre-divorce snapshots of family vacations, birthday parties, trips to Disneyland—I realized I needed to stop dwelling on the past, feeling sorry for myself, and start doing something about my future.

For the first time since the divorce, I felt like I was ready to date.

As meeting people the old-fashioned way in this town wasn't working, I figured I'd try the modern way.

The idea of dating again had been in the back of my mind from the time of my separation, but I'd ignored it. The thought of putting myself out there, going on dates, making small talk with strangers—it felt daunting.

Kayla and I had met in college. I had one steady girlfriend in high school then Kayla in college, so I had never really dated much. Especially not in the app-driven, swipe-left, swipe-right world. I felt like an unfrozen cave dweller navigating that newfound world. The thought of taking selfies, creating a profile, and advertising myself like a product on a shelf made me queasy. But the alternative—doing nothing, staying alone—felt worse. So one night, sitting in my worn, comfy recliner chair, I picked up my phone and downloaded Vibing, one of the top dating apps in the market.

I hovered over the "Create Profile" button.

How bad could it be?

TWO
ETHAN

I spent more time than I care to admit setting up my dating profile. The nerves surprised me. I was a grown man, not some high school kid fumbling through his first date. But as I stared at the screen, my fingers jittery, my palms clammy, it felt like I was going on a first date with the app itself.

I kept second-guessing everything—my photos, my bio, even my chosen interests. Should I exaggerate? No, I chided myself. I wanted to be honest. When the app presented its choices—*Casual dating. Something serious. Just seeing what's out there*—I selected casual dating. No reason to lie about it. After fifteen years in a committed relationship and eleven of those years, married, the last thing I wanted was to jump straight into another one. I was a bachelor for the first time in a very long time, so I wanted to embrace it and just have fun dating different women.

Not jump from one serious relationship into another one.

I made sure my bio was upfront. Recently divorced dad. Co-parenting my eleven-year-old son with my ex-wife. Just looking for something casual, having fun, good company, and friendly conversation. Cocktails, pool, darts, movies—let's keep it light.

When I was finally satisfied with my profile—at least, as much as I could be—I made it public.

Then I waited.

I sank into my recliner, turned on the TV, and cracked open a Diet Coke. But my eyes kept drifting toward the phone resting dark and silent on the armrest. I told myself I wouldn't check it. But after an hour with no notifications pinging, I gave in. Maybe my battery had died?

Nope. Eighty-seven percent.

My profile had a few views, but zero messages, zero matches. Crickets. I blamed the app's algorithm.

I wasn't sure what I had been expecting this soon—an instant flood of date requests? A line of eligible women in the fifty-mile radius I had selected throwing themselves at me? I shrugged it off and went to bed. First day. No big deal.

But when I woke up the next morning, the first thing I did was check my phone. I reached for it on the nightstand like a smoker going for his cancer sticks. Still nothing.

No winks, no nudges, no heart emojis.

Damn. Was I that bad looking? Maybe it was the casual dating part holding me back. Serving as a warning to the women out there that I was a horn-dog with commitment issues trolling the app for sex. I cringed at that thought. Or maybe I really wasn't cutting it in the looks department.

As I brushed my teeth, I studied my reflection in the mirror. I wasn't a model, but I wasn't some bridge troll either. I stayed lean thanks to genetics and a running habit. I had a full head of brown, wavy hair—sure, a little unkempt, but that was a style choice. My beard was neat. My honey brown eyes, from what women had told me in the past, were my best feature.

I'd even chosen a good profile picture—casual gray t-shirt, relaxed smile, nothing over the top or cringey.

So why wasn't I getting any bites?

I kept checking my phone at work. Still nothing. One of my co-workers mentioned I seemed distracted. I was too embarrassed to tell them why. Besides the embarrassment of not getting any matches, I didn't want my work colleagues to know I was on a dating app. Not sure why since it seemed many people used them.

By the time I got home from work that evening, I had mostly accepted my fate as an undatable man. Then my phone buzzed.

A match.

Finally, I thought, as I was starting to take it personally.

My heart gave an embarrassing little jolt. It was stupid, getting excited over a like on a screen, but I couldn't deny the small thrill of validation. So this was why people got addicted to those apps.

Over the next few days, my luck picked up. Seems like the app's algorithm was showing me some love. I got more likes. More matches. The dopamine hit was real from those notifications. And a few of those hits materialized into conversations that actually led somewhere.

And then, my first in-person official date.

Her name was Sheila. She was twenty-six, worked as a pet-groomer, and lived in Willow Pond, a town about fifteen miles from Fairdale. Her messages were full of emojis, and she seemed bubbly and fun.

I was nauseous from nerves.

I hadn't been on a date since I was nineteen—when Kayla and I had gone to that awful sushi place where we'd both pretended to like sea urchin. Back then, the chemistry was instant. I knew I wanted to see her again before the food even arrived.

With Sheila? Not so much.

I downplayed our eight-year age gap, but it became clear within ten minutes that age wasn't just a number—it was a chasm. She spent more time scrolling through her phone than actually engaging in conversation. When she did talk, it was about TikTok drama I didn't understand and beauty influencers I'd never heard of.

I asked about her work. "You must really love animals," I said. She looked at me, confused for a moment.

"Oh, yeah; well, not really. Dogs are fine. Just needed the job, and it's easy enough," she said. Her attention was diverted back to her phone when it pinged.

I wondered if she was texting with a friend about this terrible date with the old, boring guy or if she was back on the app looking for a better match.

By the time dinner ended, she barely made eye contact as she stood from the table.

"Nice to meet you," she said—already walking away before I could respond.

Well. That was that. There wouldn't be a second date, and I was actually relieved, though getting rejected like that did hurt my ego.

But she was right. There was no need to prolong the awkwardness. I appreciated the efficiency of her rejection at least. I paid the check, went back to my car, and drove home, feeling like a semi-truck called "online dating" had hit me.

I had naively assumed it would be like riding a bike —you never forget how to do it. But this wasn't the same bike. This was a whole new era of dating, and I was woefully out of practice.

Back home, I collapsed into my recliner. My apartment was spotless—I'd cleaned in case Sheila wanted to come over. That thought made me cringe now.

Just as I was about to turn off my phone and swear off online dating forever, it buzzed, announcing a new notification from the app.

Another match.

I picked up my phone and opened the app, my pulse kicking up. The profile belonged to a woman who looked to be in her early thirties—closer to my age.

Her name was Jade.

She had thick, glossy black hair cascading in loose waves over her shoulders and large almond-shaped eyes. Full-bodied, with well-defined cheekbones and elegantly arched brows. Striking features—a blend of softness and strength. She had the look of someone confident. Self-assured. Intriguing.

I hesitated only a moment before swiping right.

MATCH.

I grinned.

A few minutes ago, I had been ready to delete the app. Now I was completely intrigued by Jade.

THREE
ETHAN

Before heading out, I quadruple-checked myself in the mirror. I had forgotten the anxious intense state of self-consciousness dating put on its participants' shoulders.

I wore a Black Ralph Lauren polo, dark jeans, and leather sneakers. I figured the beard might not help matters, so I was clean-shaven for the first time in years. My hair was still doing its slightly unkempt thing the way I liked it. I looked presentable. Date-worthy. I sighed. Dating had also turned up the volume on those vanity feelings we like to pretend aren't inside us.

Usually, I wasn't one to obsess over my appearance, but I was in the dating trenches for the first time in a decade and a half. My first date had been a bust, so I figured I would put in a little more effort. I wondered if this one would be different.

One thing I knew—I liked Jade. At least, I liked her

on the app. We'd been chatting for a few days. She was smart. Witty. And she sounded a little wild. I could use a bit of that in my life.

But chemistry in texts and via messaging apps didn't always translate in person, as had been the case with my first date, so I was expecting the worst. I parked and glanced at myself in the rearview mirror. I really hated this part of it. I was nervous but eager to find out if this date would go down in flames like that one.

We met at the restaurant. She'd picked the place—Maggiano's, a casual but nice Italian spot in Fairdale's small downtown. I liked the choice. Italian food is always a safe bet on a first date. And the restaurant wasn't too formal yet intimate enough for a proper conversation.

I arrived five minutes early and got our table. Jade arrived exactly on time.

She looked like she did in her photos, which was a relief since I kept hearing about horror stories of folks using decades-old photos on their dating profiles.

Jade walked into the restaurant like she owned the place—black dress that suited her curvy body, high heels, waves of dark hair. Her impact seemed effortless, the kind of presence that turned heads without trying. When she saw me, her smile widened. She walked straight to the table. I began to stand, but she leaned in and kissed me lightly on the cheek, putting her hand on my shoulder for balance and gently pushing me back into my chair. She was confident. Direct. Unapologetic. I felt my entire body tingle.

She straightened up and looked down at me. "You are Ethan, right?" she said, looking at me quizzically.

My eyes widened, feeling embarrassed. "Um, yeah, I'm Ethan. Nice to meet you, Jade."

She laughed out loud, tilting her head back. It was a nice boisterous laugh that made a couple of heads turn.

"I'm screwing with you, silly," she said as she sat down. "I know it's you." She sat down across from me, making direct eye contact, which I found a bit intimidating. I've never been the most confident of men. "You're even cuter in person. That's a relief," she said.

I chuckled, adjusting the napkin in my lap. "That's something you worry about on a first date?"

"Always." She smirked. "You never know what kind of filters people use. Or if they're hiding a receding hairline with a ten-year-old photo."

The server came over. Jade asked me if I liked wine. I was more of a beer guy but drank wine too on occasions such as these. I didn't tell her all that, not wanting to sound like an uncouth bro type. "I do," I said.

Jade ordered a bottle of Napa Valley Cabernet. Her ordering a full bottle surprised me. Most people I knew played it safe with a single glass, especially on a first date. Apparently not Jade. I didn't want to sound like a prude, so I hid my surprise as best as I could.

We settled into an easy conversation while drinking wine and waiting for the food.

She told me about her job—graphic designer by day, house flipper by passion.

"I know, I know," she said, waving a hand dismissively. "I'm part of the problem. Driving up home prices, ruining America."

"So you're why I'm a renter." I smiled. "Hey, at least you're self-aware."

She laughed, taking a sip of wine. "You're not one of those guys who's going to lecture me about ethics, are you?"

"Not unless you're putting people on the street so you can tear down their homes to build a million-dollar townhouse," I said with a smile.

"Not yet."

I liked the way she leaned into sarcasm. She was sharp, always ready with a retort. A stark contrast to me—I was more measured, the type to sit back and observe before jumping in. Always trying to think what I was about to say before saying it.

But I liked how she filled the spaces I left during our conversations.

"What about graphic design?" I asked. "So you must be an artist?"

She scoffed. "I'm a whiz at Photoshop and InDesign, so I let the software do the heavy lifting. Not much to it." She waved it off. "But it paid my bills and let me get into real estate, so there's that."

Dinner flew by. I had Rigatoni Bolognese, Jade had Pasta Primavera, and we finished the bottle of wine as we flirted nonstop.

"Okay, so what's your deal?" she asked, twirling pasta onto her fork.

"My deal?"

Again she tilted her head. "You're handsome, you have a solid job, you're clearly not an idiot. So why are you single?"

I set my glass down. "Divorced."

Her eyes flickered with interest. "Saw that on your profile. How long?"

"Finalized last year."

"One kid, right?"

I nodded. "Tyler. He's eleven."

"Ah, you're a dad. Cute." She smiled. "I like dads. Means you're responsible. Stable."

"I'd like to think so." I chuckled.

"No crazy-ex drama?"

I hesitated, then shook my head. "Nope. Kayla and I actually get along pretty well, for Tyler's sake."

"Why didn't it work out?"

"We just... weren't meant to last. No big drama. We just grew apart, so went our separate ways. Well, as separate as we can get, sharing a child."

Jade leaned back, considering me. "Huh."

"What?" I asked, sounding more defensive than I wanted.

"Most men aren't that emotionally aware. They'd just say she was a bitch and call it a day."

"I guess I'm not most men," I said with a small laugh.

"No, Ethan, I don't think you are."

I blushed. "Okay, my turn. Do you have kids?"

Her expression shifted slightly, just enough for me to notice.

"Two. A boy and a girl. They live with their father in Portland."

That was interesting. Usually, kids stay with their mother, even nowadays.

"Well, Portland isn't too far away at least. A few hundred miles from Fairdale?"

"Portland, Maine, actually," she said, taking the longest sip of wine of our date.

That was coast to coast. Over 3,000 miles away. Even flying out there meant around a ten-hour flight, one-way. I could never imagine being that far from Tyler. Seven hundred miles was too far, hence my being up here on this date.

But it wasn't my business, even though it struck me as... unusual. I didn't want to judge.

I noticed her demeanor shifted. The playful, boisterous energy she'd carried all evening faded, replaced by something quieter. Darker.

"Let's just say that, unlike you, my ex," she said, swirling her wine, "is a bitch, and I'm calling it a day."

Then, just as quickly, she lifted her glass. "Enough about exes. Here's to the future."

I clinked my glass against hers. She downed her wine in one sip.

"Chin-chin," she said loudly, making a few heads turn.

After dinner, neither of us was ready to call it a night. So we agreed to change it up and hit a good old dive bar.

"I know just the place," Jade said.

She led me a few blocks away to Bigfoot's, a Fairdale institution: neon beer signs, old license plates on the walls, a couple of pool tables in the back. The smell of beer and fried food lingered in the air, and a country song played softly from the jukebox.

"Hey, Jade," the bartender called out.

"How's it hanging, Ernie?" she asked.

"To the left, as usual."

A few regulars chuckled. Jade grinned.

I stood there awkwardly. Jade also seemed to be a regular.

"Ever been here?" she asked.

"No. I haven't really explored much around town yet," I said. It just dawned on me what a hermit I had been since moving here. I kept complaining how hard it was to meet people in Fairdale, yet I had failed to set foot inside a popular bar in town, until tonight.

"Well, you're in for a treat," she said, smiling. "Bigfoot's is the best bar in town. A little grimy. The pool tables wobble, but they make up for it with cheap liquor." She turned to the bartender, who stood there with a smirk.

"Two deer and beers, Ernie." She tapped the bar lightly without asking me if I liked that drink.

I wasn't a fan of Jägermeister. The German herbal liqueur didn't sit well with me after I'd gotten too drunk off it as a teenager. Ernie set a pint of cold beer and a shot of Jägermeister in front of Jade and then me.

Jade picked up the shot glass and raised it. Back in LA, that would be considered a double shot. I swallowed hard, picked up my shot glass and held it up to hers.

"To new friends," she said with a wide smile. That toast loosened me up, and I also smiled. "To new friends," I repeated. Our glasses clicked, and she took the shot in one gulp. Then she took a big drink of beer. It took me two embarrassed tries to down the Jägermeister. I cleared my throat and took a sip of beer, feeling the warm liqueur and cold beer rumbling inside my stomach. Before I could say anything, Jade tapped on the bar, a little harder this time. "Another round, Ernie."

I wanted to wave her off. But I caved to the peer pressure and repeated the drill. Between the wine, beer, and liqueur, I was feeling fuzzy. The way she looked at me, I was pretty sure how this night was going to end. I smiled and licked my lips in anticipation.

Before I knew it, Jade jumped out of her chair. "Let's shoot some pool," she said, heading towards the back of the bar with a pint of beer in her hand. I followed along noticing how lightheaded I felt.

We found an empty table, and Jade immediately racked up the balls.

"You play?"

"A little."

She arched an eyebrow. "A little, huh?"

I smiled. "Why? You a shark?"

Eyes locked on mine, she leaned in. "Wouldn't you like to know?"

Turns out, Jade was a shark.

I struggled to keep up. Meanwhile, she played with a casual, effortless confidence—sinking shots like it was second nature.

By the time we stumbled out of Bigfoot's, we were drunk, arm in arm, laughing, swaying on the sidewalk.

"Well," I said, "I don't think either of us should drive."

Jade pulled out her phone. "I'll order us an Uber," she said.

"Love to share an Uber with you," I said, feeling my knees wobbly. "I'll give you my address so you can put in as the second address."

She looked at me with soft, shining eyes and a thin smile.

"We just need one stop. Wanna come over to my place?"

I met her gaze—wide, open, unguarded, which made me feel nervous. She leaned in and kissed me on the lips. A long, deep, sensual kiss that set my knees shaking.

We came apart, and she looked at me as no woman had in a long time, and it felt so good.

The words caught for a second before I managed, "Let's go to your place."

FOUR
ETHAN

I woke up before Jade. Sunlight filtered through the blinds, brightening the room. I lay for a moment, listening to her steady breathing and feeling her warmth beside me.

It had been a long time since I'd woken up next to anyone other than Kayla. Fifteen years, to be exact.

Most of my adult life had been spent with one woman: Kayla. I'd never casually hooked up with anyone before, so to say I had no experience in this department was putting it mildly. Jade was only the fourth woman I'd ever slept with. And none of them—not even Kayla—had been like Jade.

Jade was wild, in bed, on the kitchen floor, and even on the couch in her living room. She was uninhibited in a way that left my head spinning. She did things Kayla never had. But it wasn't just the sex. It was the way she moved, the way she took control, the way she made me feel like she'd been waiting for me—not just someone, but me. I ran a hand through my hair and sat up quietly, my movements slow so I wouldn't wake her.

My head throbbed, my mouth was dry. I felt dehydrated. Not just from the earth-shattering sex, but from the sheer amount of alcohol I'd consumed last night. I wasn't a big drinker. A couple of beers, a glass of wine with dinner—that was my usual speed, not drinking a bottle of wine and slamming deer and beers all night. I hadn't drunk that much in years, and I was paying for it now with a dry mouth and pounding headache. But as I watched Jade lying next to me in bed, I smiled. It was worth it.

I glanced at the clock. 7:42 a.m.

Kayla was dropping off Tyler at my apartment at 10:00. That gave me just enough time to get home, shower, chug a gallon of water, clean up, and not look like I was death warmed over before they arrived.

I turned toward Jade. She lay on her side, the sheets tangled around her, her dark hair spilling over the pillow. In sleep, she looked softer, almost delicate—a far cry from the confident, head-turning force she had been last night. I wondered what it would be like to stay in bed with her all morning. Having breakfast together. Morning sex, perhaps.

But I couldn't even consider that since I had Tyler coming over. Besides, I didn't want to send Jade the wrong message. I had been honest with her from the start. During our chat and text messages and at the restaurant when we first met, I'd made it clear I wasn't looking for anything serious. This was a casual date. A hook up. Nothing more than that. And she had agreed to that. Told me that's what she wanted for too — just out to hang out and have fun. And that we did.

I slipped out of bed, started gathering my clothes and got dressed. I had just finished buttoning my jeans when Jade stirred. I turned towards her.

She blinked a few times, then smiled faintly. "Hey," she said with a yawn.

"Hey," I said back to her, pulling my shirt over my head.

Her eyes roamed over me, slow and lazy, a satisfied smirk playing on her lips. "You're up early. It's Saturday."

"Yeah, I, uh..." I hesitated, feeling like a douche. "I've got to get home. Kayla's dropping off Tyler soon."

For a split second, something flickered across her face. A shift—small, but noticeable. She wasn't happy with my response.

"Right," she said, her tone light. "Of course."

She pushed herself up on one elbow; the sheets slipped lower on her body, exposing her breasts. She did not cover herself.

She gave me an impish smile. Her half-lidded eyes and bare breasts tempted me to crawl back into bed for more of her wildness.

I swallowed hard and licked my dry lips. "I have to go," I managed to say.

"I was hoping we could hang out today." She stretched, her movements slow and deliberate. "Maybe get breakfast." Then she shrugged, like it was nothing. "But... another time, maybe?"

Jade was playing it off, but something about the way she'd spoken made me pause. Her tone was casual, but her expression wasn't. Or maybe I was imagining it. I had no experience in this type of casual hook up.

Yet I wanted to see her again. She was a lot of fun. And who knows where things might lead? My bravado in only looking for casual dating might go right out the window. But I couldn't think about any of that right now. I had to get home to my son.

I smiled at her. "Yeah, another time for sure."

She watched as I grabbed my jacket.

"Last night was fun," she said, another smirk curling the edge of her lips.

"It was," I agreed. I felt my cheeks flush.

She tilted her head. "So we should do it again, right?"

I grinned. "Absolutely."

Her smile widened, but her eyes didn't smile along.

She pushed the covers back, sliding out of bed naked in a slow, deliberate movement. She didn't put clothes on, just walked over to me and wrapped her arms around my neck, pulling me in for a slow, lingering kiss.

"Call me," she murmured against my lips.

I could hardly breathe. "I will."

Running my hands down her bare arms, I pulled back. Although we had spent the evening having sex and she was pressing up against my dressed body, I kept my eyes on hers as if to look down and take in her nakedness would be rude. I sighed and kissed her forehead.

"I'll be in touch," I said wistfully.

Then, reluctantly, I left.

THE MORNING AIR was crisp and cool as I stepped outside. The street was quiet, lined with parked cars. A jogger passed me, giving me a look like she knew what I had been doing, but I shrugged. How would she know? *I'm projecting.* Like I wanted to stand on the corner of the street yelling like a proselytizing street preacher: *I just had sex with Jade Sommer.* I snickered over my silliness. I looked for my car, remembered I'd left it at the restaurant, and pulled out my phone to order an Uber.

It only took a few minutes for a white Toyota Camry with the ride-sharing decal on its window to pull up. As I slid into the car, I glanced up at Jade's bedroom window.

The blinds were closed.

I shook my head, snickering at myself.

What was I expecting? For her to be standing there, watching me with desire? Eagerly waving at me?

I was overthinking things, as usual. Jade was fun. And like we had agreed, this was just casual.

I couldn't stop smiling. My first dating app conquest—I felt ten feet tall.

"Good night?" the driver asked, snapping me out of my daze.

I glanced over. He wore a shit-eating grin, like he already knew the answer.

"Not too shabby," I said, grinning back.

He chuckled and pulled away from the curb.

As I leaned back in the seat, I caught the dumb grin still plastered across my face on the reflection in the window. I looked like a teenager who had just got lucky for the first time.

I couldn't wait to see Jade again.

FIVE
JADE

I climbed back to bed and watched Ethan leave. As soon as I heard the door click shut, I stretched, my body still warm from the night before. I reached for the sheets and buried my face in them. They smelled like him. Like us. A hint of cologne, a lingering trace of sweat, the sweet undertone of the shampoo I'd used yesterday. I inhaled deeply, memorizing the scent, locking it away like a precious secret.

His footsteps faded down the hallway towards the front door, each step becoming quieter, more distant. A faint thud signaled him picking up his shoes, slipping them back on by the door. The muffled jingling of keys followed, a subtle yet sharp reminder he was leaving. Then the finality of the front door opening and closing reverberated through the silence, a soft, dull click echoing in my heart. Instantly, I felt so alone.

For a moment, I didn't move. I remained curled

beneath the sheets, cocooned in warmth, clinging to the last traces of his presence. I won't lie: I had hoped he would stay. At least for breakfast, at least for coffee. But I had seen it clearly in his face earlier—the moment he decided to leave. The shift had been subtle yet unmistakable. His smile had tightened at the edges, his eyes glancing briefly toward the window, searching for the best way to make his gentle exit. He let me down softly, skillfully, making it almost impossible for me to argue or feel justified in my disappointment. I know that when choosing between me and his son, he would pick his son every day of the week and twice on Sunday. Even so, I felt the sting of rejection, and it hurt.

But he hadn't completely closed the door on us. Another time. Maybe he had said it when I asked if he'd like to meet up again. The ambiguity of his answer lingered in my thoughts like an unsolved puzzle. Another time. Was that genuine hope or merely a polite dismissal?

Feeling restless, I slid out from beneath the covers and walked toward the window, not bothering to grab a robe. The cool air brushed against my bare skin, raising goosebumps along my arms. My footsteps whispered softly on the wooden floor, an intimate, lonely sound in the quiet room.

I stood behind the closed blinds, listening carefully, almost hopefully, for something—anything—to indicate he hadn't left yet. Silence stretched on for a few heartbeats, then faint shuffling feet on the pavement reached my ears, and the muted rumble of an approaching car broke through the stillness.

My heart gave a tiny leap of anticipation. Was he hesitating? Was he coming back inside to say goodbye properly, maybe to tell me he'd changed his mind and ask to stay longer? I reached up slowly, sliding two fingers between the slats, careful not to move the blinds too obviously. Through the narrow opening, I could see him clearly, outlined by the early morning sunlight, standing beside the car now idling at the curb. My heart sank a little.

Ethan climbed into the car, his broad shoulders easing back against the seat, his head tilted back as if he were already thinking of something—or someone—else. A faint ache tightened in my chest, a sharp, uncomfortable pang of insecurity and regret.

I silently willed him to glance up at my window, to give me one final, reassuring look. Just one. But his attention remained fixed forward, his hand reaching up to smooth his tousled hair as he settled into the seat. He said something to the driver, a brief exchange punctuated by a laugh that made me feel strangely excluded. A wave of jealousy hit me, irrational and quick. I wondered if he was laughing about me—about us. Had it all been a joke to him? Was I merely a funny story he'd share with friends later?

I forced myself to shake off those destructive thoughts, watching helplessly as the car pulled away and disappeared down the street. I stayed at the window long after it was gone, eyes fixated on the now empty road, my mind racing with a thousand questions and doubts.

He was going to call me. He said he would. And despite everything, despite the nagging uncertainty coiled deep in my chest, I believed him. He seemed too genuine, too gentle, to lie outright. Yet there was something off—something in his voice earlier this morning, something about the guarded way he smiled and looked at me, as though he were trying to hide an unspoken truth about our hook up.

It was fine, though. I had no right to expect anything more. Ethan had been completely honest with me from the start. He'd said clearly he was freshly divorced and craving freedom, wanting to sow his wild oats after years of marriage, not looking for anything serious. I'd agreed willingly, eagerly even, desperate for excitement after a long stretch of loneliness. We both got what we wanted.

The slats clicked back into place, the sudden sound loud in the quiet room. Yet, as I turned away from the window, a slow smile formed on my lips. I knew I had rocked his world last night. I'd seen it in his wide-eyed, amazed expression—the slight tremor of his hands, the breathless laughter that broke from his chest when he pretended he'd done this before. It had been clear from the beginning that he wasn't the most experienced lover. And oddly enough, I found that charming. Endearing. Sweet.

I wanted to see him again. That much I knew for certain. Whatever it took, whatever he needed to feel comfortable, I would give it to him. I'd be patient if I had to. Wait for him to realize that this wasn't just casual fun—this could be something real. Something special. He just needed time.

And patience was something I had plenty of.

I glanced around the lonely room, letting the lingering warmth and scent of Ethan fill me with hope. We'd see each other again soon.

I'd make sure of it.

SIX
ETHAN

I couldn't stop thinking about Jade. It was the most fun I'd had in a very long time. For sure since I'd moved to Fairdale.

So I put aside worries that I would send her mixed messages by seeing her again. I put the ball in her court. If she was okay seeing me in a non-exclusive way, and she was good with that, then why not? I called her the very next day.

For the first few weeks, Jade and I couldn't keep our hands off each other. We went out often, drinking at Bigfoot's, trying new restaurants, going on long late-night drives that always ended with us tangled up together in bed, on the couch, on the floor—wherever we happened to land first. We even did it in the car like a pair of lusty teenagers.

The sex was wild. Hot. Heavy. Relentless. She took me out to Whitehall Park to an isolated overlook carved out of the Fernwood National Forest. Down the Redwood Grove Trail, then off the beaten path into a clearing amid the woods. We made love on the forest ground at dusk like a couple of wild forest animals.

She was uninhibited in a way that thrilled me, open in ways the other women I'd known never were. She had no shame about her sexuality, something that I'd struggled with my whole life. But Jade had no hesitation, no limits.

It was intoxicating, like discovering something new about myself at thirty-four — something raw and primal deep inside I didn't even know I had until she brought it out.

Jade made me feel wanted like I hadn't felt in years.

I had even brought her to one of my happy hours after work, where she met some of my colleagues. She was cheerful and nice, and having a good time. It seemed everyone had a good time around Jade.

And at first I saw no problem with it.

But after a while, I started wondering if I was sending the wrong message. I was enjoying my time with Jade, but my attraction to her was physical only.

Jade said she wanted nothing serious either, but... something in the way she looked at me sometimes made me question that. The last thing I wanted was to play with someone's emotions.

One Friday night, she texted: *Bigfoot's tonight?*

I had Tyler the next morning and needed to get

some sleep. So for the first time, I turned her down. *Can't tonight. Long day, and I've got my son tomorrow.*

She didn't respond right away. When she finally did, it was with one letter: *K.*

Different from her usual style, but I brushed it off. The next day at work, a colleague told me Jade had been at Bigfoot's that night, drinking hard, laughing loudly, flirting with the bartender. Having a good time without me, so perhaps I was reading too much into it. She was fine.

I had gone a few days without seeing her when my phone buzzed at ten p.m. It was Jade.

Jade: *You up?*

I was. So I texted her back.

Ethan: *Yeah.*

Jade: *Booty call?*

That took me aback. I could feel a saucy grin spread on my face. I stared at my phone for a moment, then typed back: *Come over.*

Jade: *BRT*

I jumped out of my recliner, ran into my bedroom, and straightened the sheets. Next, I ran to the bathroom, brushed my teeth and rinsed with mouthwash. I checked myself in the mirror and made sure I looked decent, since I hadn't been expecting company.

Less than five minutes later, Jade arrived. She must have been really close. Fairdale was small, but she lived on the outskirts of town, in the opposite direction of my apartment.

I buzzed her in, opened the door and waited for her there. I saw her pop up from the stairway landing as she made her way down a long corridor. My apartment was the last one on that floor, so I watched her walk towards me with a smile, my anticipation about what was about to happen off the charts.

Jade grinned as she walked inside, saying nothing, wearing a long coat. I closed the door, and she opened her coat like a flasher to show that underneath she wore a silky, sexy negligee.

"Wow," was all I could muster as I leaned back into the door.

She flung herself at me, kissing me, our hands all over each other's bodies. We hadn't spoken a word, just emitted gasps when we stopped kissing to catch our breaths before starting again as we made our way into the bedroom.

Afterward, she curled up next to me in bed, tracing circles on my chest with her nails.

"I could get used to this," she murmured.

I chuckled. "Yeah?"

She tilted her head up at me. "Would that be so bad?"

I wasn't sure how to answer that. Instead, I kissed her, and we did it again.

A FEW DAYS LATER, we went out for drinks. Jade got drunker than usual, clinging to me, her hands always on me, pulling me closer. When I said I had to leave, she blocked my path, arms spread wide.

"No," she said, laughing, but her eyes didn't match her tone. "You can't leave yet."

"Jade," I said lightly. "Come on."

She grabbed my shirt, balling it into her fists. "Stay."

I frowned. "I've got work in the morning."

She rolled her eyes, laughing like it was a joke, but I could feel the tension in her grip.

Finally, she let go, raising her hands in surrender. "Fine, fine. You're no fun."

THE NEXT DAY SHE APOLOGIZED, saying she'd been drunk, that she was just messing around.

And maybe she was. But something about the way she hadn't wanted to let me go made me feel... uneasy.

I liked Jade, but I knew she wasn't the girl for me in the long term. So I figured it was time to cool things off with her. I didn't want to mess with her on an emotional level. Even though she kept telling me she was okay with keeping things casual, I no longer believed that was true.

I was going through the Vibing app when I saw the profile of a woman that got my interest.

Her name was Laura, a teacher. She seemed a bit more my speed than Jade.

A few days later, we met for coffee. It was fine. But

she wasn't Jade. And even though I told myself that's what I was looking for, I felt a longing for that wild side. There was also no spark, no undeniable heat between Laura and me.

After the date, I knew I wouldn't see her again. I sat in my car, thinking about Jade. Before I could stop myself, I sent her a message.

Ethan: *What are you up to?*

Her response came immediately.

Jade: *Come over.*

So I did.

And when I left a few hours later, I felt... guilty. Like I was using her. Perhaps I'd been lying to myself all along about what this was between Jade and me.

A FEW DAYS LATER, Kayla made a comment.

"You've been busy lately," she said casually as we sat in the kitchen watching Tyler eat his mac and cheese.

I took a sip of water. "Not really."

She lifted an eyebrow. "You haven't asked to keep Tyler overnight for a while."

I frowned. "That's not true."

She smirked. "Uh, yeah. It is."

I scratched my jaw. "I've just had some stuff to do."

Kayla crossed her arms. She looked at me suspiciously. "Stuff? Or someone?"

I exhaled. "I signed up for a dating app."

She blinked. "No way. You?"

I chuckled. "Yeah, me."

She shook her head. "God. That's so weird."

We both laughed, and for a second it felt almost like old times.

"I promise I'll spend more time with Tyler," I said.

She nodded, her expression softer now. "Good."

THAT NIGHT, back in my apartment, I thought about my feelings for Jade. What I felt for Jade was lust, and that was it. You can't build a relationship on such a flimsy foundation. I had to stop leading Jade on like this. It wasn't fair to her, me, or my son. So I sent her a text.

Hey. So things are getting a little busy for me. I've got a lot going on with work and Tyler. So I won't be able to hang out with you anymore.

There was a long pause before she responded.

Jade: *K.*

That was it.

Just like before.

I frowned at the screen. Shit. I should have called her to talk about this. I've just gotten so wrapped into this damn mobile device for everything except making a phone call like it was designed to do from the start.

Ethan: *You okay?*

Another long pause. Then she replied.

Yeah. Of course. I told you. I'm okay with this being casual. That is what you want, right?

I kept my reply simple: *Yes.*

Jade: *All good, then.*

I could hear the hurt in her short, clipped responses.

But I didn't reply, though I felt terrible. I figured making a clean break was the best way forward.

SEVEN
ETHAN

A WEEK HAD PASSED SINCE I'D LAST SEEN JADE. I hadn't texted her. Not once during that time.

It wasn't easy. My mind drifted to her more often than I wanted to admit—not out of affection or love but lust. And I felt terrible about it. But I couldn't get those memories out of my head. The way she kissed, the way she touched me, the way she made me feel wanted in a way I hadn't felt in years. But I knew I had to keep my distance. It wasn't right for me to toy with her emotions for my selfish needs, although she kept insisting she was fine with our non-exclusive casual dating.

She had reached out to me a few times over text messages, but I'd turned her down, telling her it wasn't a good idea for us to see each other anymore.

Still, as I sat doomscrolling Netflix on a Friday night without really watching anything, I felt... bored.

Restless. I still had the Vibing app on my phone, so

I figured, what the hell. I grabbed my phone from the coffee table and opened the app.

I scrolled through profiles absentmindedly, swiping left more often than right. Too young. Too old. Not my type.

Then my thumb froze. I got a closer look at the photo looking back at me. I recognized that face. I couldn't believe it. This was someone I knew in real life. I blinked and enlarged the image as much as I could, making sure I wasn't imagining things. The profile username Christina G. There was no doubt: I knew her. It was Christina Garza.

I sat up straighter. No way. What are the odds of running into a profile of someone you had met offline? I had no idea if that was common or not, but I found it weird. And exhilarating.

When I met her at work, I found her attractive. Long, thick brown hair. Dark eyes that held sharp intelligence. High cheekbones and full lips.

She was a manager in the finance department at the company I worked for. I'd only been at Fitzek Manufacturing for a couple of weeks when she left for a huge promotion at another company. She was barely thirty, and she had already landed a finance director position; that was impressive. I figured she was very smart and good at her job, but I hadn't known her well before she left and hadn't seen her since. We'd spoken a handful of times about mostly work-related things. Her laptop had been dragging; I'd taken a look and suggested in a friendly, teasing voice that the reason for her slow computer was the dozens upon dozens of applications she had open and running at one time.

"You're a running-app hoarder, huh?" I said with a grin. She blushed, and we shared a chuckle. She was always polite but professional. Way out of my league.

Yet, there she was. On Vibing.

I had an internal debate. Should I? Was it creepy to have an ex-colleague reach out on a dating app? I hesitated for a second, feeling awkward about it—but if she was on the app, she was interested in dating. And her profile said she was straight, looking to connect with men. I fit the bill. So why not? I swiped right.

And then I really double-downed—I sent her a direct message: *Hey! I know you!*

I set my phone down, not expecting much. She probably wouldn't even see it. Or she would swipe left at the creepy IT guy hitting on her.

An hour later, I was half-asleep in my recliner chair watching *Blue Bloods* when my phone buzzed with a notification. I glanced over at it and immediately pepped up at seeing the notification.

Christina matched with you!

My heart jumped, surprising me. Then a message popped up. She'd replied to my DM. I sat up.

Christina: *I remember you! You work at Fitzek Manufacturing, right? The IT guy that app-shamed me?*

I grinned. I couldn't believe she remembered me.

Ethan: *That's right. It was a you-have-too-many-open-apps-at-once intervention! You left Fitzek a couple of weeks after I started. Fancy running into you on an app, of all places.*

She replied almost instantly.

Christina: *Small world. So, still shutting down apps and resetting passwords?*

Ethan: *Living the dream.*

Christina: *Sounds thrilling.*

Ethan: *Oh, you wouldn't believe the excitement.*

She sent back a laughing emoji.

It was flirty. Playful. We had only exchanged a few silly messages, but I felt at ease with her already.

And just like that, we started talking more and more.

OVER THE NEXT couple of days, Christina and I texted back and forth constantly.

At work. Late at night. During lunch breaks.

I found myself checking my phone more often, smiling when I saw a notification from her. She was smart and quick-witted, but also funnier than I'd expected.

She had a dry, sarcastic humor I liked. I was certain she had grown up with a few brothers, the way she rolled with being teased and dishing it back all in fun.

Ethan: *Tell me, do finance directors actually do any work, or just sit in meetings all day?*

Christina: *98% meetings. 2% approving expense reports. And yes, I'm exhausted at the end of the day.*

Ethan: *Sounds brutal. I'll stick to tech support.*

Christina: *Are foot rubs at the end of a long day part of tech support?*

I liked where this was going.

Ethan: *You bet. I got my foot massage technique down to a T. Not even a tickle.*

Christina: *Sure. I bet you just browse Reddit all day and pretend to be busy, anyway.*

Ethan: *Please, I mix it up with some YouTube too.*

She sent a laughing GIF.

It was effortless.

Unlike with Jade, where everything had been fast, intense, overwhelming, this was... different. This felt normal.

I liked that feeling. I liked her.

Two DAYS LATER, as I lay in bed, scrolling through my messages with her, I took the plunge.

Ethan: *I have a crazy idea.*

Christina: *Uh-oh.*

Ethan: *What if instead of texting each other all day, we actually meet in person?*

She left me on read for a minute.

I exhaled, feeling stupid for asking.

Then—

Christina: *So, like a real date?*

Ethan: *A real date. What do you think?*

Christina: *Hmm... risky move, but I'm intrigued.*

Ethan: *I'll take intrigued over a flat-out no.*

Christina: *Alright, Mr. IT, where are you taking me?*

I grinned.

Ethan: *How about dinner?*

Christina: *Dinner works.*

Ethan: *Any preferences?*

Christina: *Surprise me.*

Ethan: *Challenge accepted.*

I set my phone down, grinning like an idiot.

For the first time in weeks, I felt genuinely excited about a date.

Cooling things off with Jade had been the right call. This was the type of feeling that I hadn't had with her.

Christina lived in Whitlock, a town smaller and more rural than Fairdale, located ten miles away. We settled on a Thai restaurant in Fairdale, since her town didn't have any restaurants. Not even a McDonald's.

When I offered to pick her up, she said it was silly to drive ten miles out there then turn around and drive ten miles back to Fairdale.

It was nice of her to be so thoughtful. We agreed to meet at the Jasmine Lotus restaurant.

I got there early and grabbed a table by the window, letting the staff know I was on a first date. They were all smiles.

She was running late. No biggie. Then ten minutes passed. No Christina. I wondered if she would stand me up. It had happened once before on another Vibing date. The woman had then ghosted me.

But my phone buzzed.

Christina: *Sorry, I'm late. Be there in 5.*

I exhaled, relieved.

A few minutes later, I saw a shiny new black BMW 4 Series Gran Coupe pull into the parking lot.

Nice car, I thought. BMWs weren't as common in these parts as they were down in Los Angeles. The little insecure voice inside my head reminded me once again: *She's way out of your league.*

She walked past the window and caught me staring like an excited puppy with its nose on the glass. She smiled at me and I turned red. I gave her a half wave. *Get it together, Ethan.*

I got up to greet her. Hug? Handshake? Kiss on the cheek? I hate this part of the first date. We ended up in one of those weird half-hugs, then settled into our seats. Luckily, that initial awkwardness soon dissipated, and soon after she sat down, the conversation between us flowed effortlessly.

We drank Singha beers, shared chicken satay, spring rolls, Pad Thai, and green curry.

We talked about work, life, our pasts.

She was thirty and had been married young, like me. She also had a son, but his father lived in San Francisco and wasn't in the picture much.

I could tell she didn't want to dwell on it, so I didn't push.

Midway through dinner, my phone buzzed. It had been doing that all night, much to my embarrassment.

I glanced at my phone to make sure it was an emergency. They had all been sent by Jade.

My phone buzzed as I held it. Jade, again. I silenced it quickly, but Christina noticed.

She smiled, taking a sip of beer. "Another Vibing match?"

I felt my face heat up.

"No," I said. "It's—complicated."

"Ooh, interesting. Tell me more," she said with a wide grin.

She must have seen how embarrassed I had become because she laughed.

"I'm only teasing. It's none of my business. You've been honest that you're only interested in casual dating. Me too. So don't worry about it."

"Thanks. It's just... I feel like a heel."

She leaned in slightly and smiled. "Don't. It's what I'm looking for in my busy, hectic life.. I just want to have fun."

"You do?" I said, not sounding convinced. Sure she says that now, but after?

"Scout's honor. I'm happy to pull a Lauper," she added.

"What's a Lauper?"

"Cyndi Lauper. 'Girls Just Want to Have Fun.'"

I laughed. She was too good to be true.

We left the restaurant and I walked her to her car. I felt so at ease and relaxed with Christina, as if we were on the same page on everything, that I didn't even start overthinking whether I should try to make a move. I just leaned in and kissed her, and she kissed me back. Our first kiss was blissful. We made out by her car for a couple of minutes. We were both breathless when I told her my apartment was only a couple miles away and invited her over. She smiled.

"I'll follow you in my car."

EIGHT
ETHAN

Christina and I walked into my apartment kissing, our bodies intertwined. I shoved the door closed with my foot.

I tried to ask her if she wanted anything to drink, but she kept kissing me as she pressed her body against mine. Her arms were over my shoulders as she kissed me, deep and slow. Her fingers slid into the back of my hair, her nails grazing my scalp as she tilted my head slightly, deepening the kiss.

My hands instinctively moved to her back, pressing against the soft fabric of her blouse. She felt incredible. Warm. Eager.

I had no idea how far I should take this, but then she pressed her body against me even closer than before and I felt her hips roll, just enough for me to know she wanted this as badly as I did.

This was really going to happen. I had silenced my cell phone earlier to keep from getting distracted, so when my landline suddenly rang, the shrill sound cut through the room like a gunshot. I couldn't remember the last time that thing had rung.

We both jumped, startled. Then she started laughing.

"Is that a landline?" she asked me, sounding genuinely curious that I would have this old-fashioned phone from yesteryear hooked up.

It was a landline phone. The only reason I even had one was for Tyler.

I cursed under my breath. Of all the times... "Yeah, I keep a landline for emergencies so my son can reach me if my cell phone is out or something."

Christina let out a breathy laugh, stepping back and brushing a strand of hair behind her ear. "You should probably get that."

"Yeah... Sorry." I went to the kitchen, checked my cell—no missed calls or texts from Kayla. Just a bunch of unread text messages from Jade. I ignored those. Who could be calling me at this time on that number, I wondered as I picked up the receiver.

"Hello?" I answered, unable to hide the annoyance in my voice.

"Hey, handsome."

My stomach dropped.

It was Jade. I closed my eyes briefly, my jaw tightening. Why on earth would she be calling me this late and on that number? I didn't even remember giving that number to her.

I turned slightly, glancing at Christina. She was scrolling on her phone, giving me space, completely unaware of what was unfolding.

"Why are you calling me this late on my landline?" I asked quietly.

"I couldn't reach you on your cell, so thought I'd try you on the old relic. And hey, it worked," she said.

"Why are you calling me so late?"

Jade giggled. "What do you think? Booty call, silly."

I clenched my teeth. God, this was awkward.

Reminding myself that I had always been honest with both Jade and Christina, I took a deep breath. Casual dating. No exclusivity. I wasn't cheating. I wasn't playing games.

Still, this felt... wrong.

I cleared my throat. "Listen, Jade, I'm sorry, but now's not a good time. I have company."

There was a pause on the other end.

Then: "Who's there?"

I exhaled sharply. I wouldn't sugarcoat things. "I'm on a date."

Silence.

Then her tone changed. "Well, I'm downstairs."

"What?"

"Yeah. I was coming over to rock your night, but I also left something at your place, and I need it."

I pinched the bridge of my nose, feeling my pulse tick against my fingertips.

"You can't be serious. Tell me what it is, and I'll drop it off at your place tomorrow."

"That doesn't work for me." Her voice was clipped now, annoyed. "I need it right away. And I'm here. What's the big deal? We're all adults. I'm sure you told her about casual dating too, right?"

She was always cool, laid-back—at least, that's how she had always presented herself to me, and now this? She sounded entitled to showing up unannounced and demanding things. Like she had a right to be here.

"It will only take a minute," she said. "I'm already here."

I sighed. "Hold on a second."

Christina had set her phone down and was watching me with mild curiosity. I was mortified.

Before I could say anything, she stood up, smoothing her blouse. "Sounds like you have your hands full tonight. I better go home."

"No, Christina, you don't have to do that." I shook my head, stepping toward her. "It's just a girl I've been seeing... but I haven't dated her in a couple of weeks. She left something here, that's all. She won't stay long."

I felt pathetic for apologizing so much, but I hated that this was happening.

She studied me for a moment, then smiled—not mad, not upset, just... understanding.

Stepping forward, she cupped my face in her hands and kissed me gently.

"You don't have to apologize, Ethan." She pulled back just slightly, her lips still hovering over mine. "I knew from the first time I messaged you on the app that this wasn't exclusive. We're both dating other people on the app. It's fine."

I was relieved but still uneasy.

She leaned in and whispered, "I tell you what. Once you're done here, and if you're game, come over to my house tonight."

"Yeah?"

"My son is staying with my mom tonight. So I'll be home alone. Come on over if you want." She smiled.

I smiled back and told her I would be delighted to stop over shortly.

Then I walked Christina down the flight of stairs to the front door of my apartment complex.

If it weren't for the electronic key-code entry, I was certain that Jade would have been banging on my apartment door already.

Instead, she stood just outside the double glass doors, peering inside like a bill collector, arms crossed.

The yellow glow from the overhead light gave her face a muted, almost washed-out look, making it hard to read her expression.

My nerves tightened. This was so awkward. I'd

never juggled two women simultaneously like this before. Even though I had been transparent with both about my intentions and I had stopped seeing Jade, I felt like a double-timing, cheating, dirty dog.

I pushed open the door.

Jade stepped aside, leaning against the wall, arms still crossed. She looked at me and then she turned towards Christina, giving her the once-over as she walked out.

For the briefest moment, they locked eyes. But Jade quickly turned away, looking down at the ground.

Neither said a word to the other. Not even a quick hello.

I glanced from one to the other, suddenly aware of how tense the air felt.

In terms of traditional beauty standards, Christina was the clear winner—polished, elegant, effortlessly stunning.

Jade had a softer, curvier look; still beautiful, but in a different way.

And for a second, I felt a flicker of something ridiculous: pride.

These two good-looking women wanted me.

Then reality hit me like a slap.

Jade had shown up unannounced, at 10:30 at night, ruining my date with Christina.

That wasn't sexy. That wasn't flattering.

That was a problem.

I turned back to Jade, suddenly irritated.

"I'll be right back," I muttered curtly.

She raised an eyebrow, as if she found my frustration amusing.

Christina shot me a small, understanding smile before walking away.

I could feel Jade watching as I walked Christina to her BMW. She climbed in. And I apologized again.

"No need. Come over tonight, okay?"

"I'll be there," I said with a wide smile.

She drove away. But I had committed; no matter what I had to do, I was going to get rid of Jade so I could get over to Christina's place as quickly as possible.

As I walked back towards Jade, I felt angry at her. How dare she?

"BMW. Puts my Subaru to shame, huh?"

I didn't answer, nor did I acknowledge what she'd said.

"Well, come on up, I suppose. Make it quick," I said. I was being rude, but I'd had it with Jade.

"I'm sorry, Ethan, I just really need my notebook. I didn't realize we wouldn't be seeing each other in such a long time. Otherwise, I wouldn't have left it here."

I regretted having picked up the phone.

Jade walked inside and I stayed a few steps behind her as she went up the stairs and into the hallway, heading towards my apartment. Something about her presence felt different tonight—heavier, more invasive.

The clicking of her heels against the stairs created a loud, unnatural echo in the stairwell.

"So, what exactly did you leave here?" I asked, trying to keep my tone neutral and not reveal how annoyed I was about her ruining my date.

"My sketchbook. The one with all my property renovation plans. I need it for a house I'm renovating to flip. I have a meeting with the construction foreman in the morning," she explained. Then she glanced back at me, her smile not quite reaching her eyes. "It's probably in your bedroom."

I hadn't seen any sketchbooks in my apartment, and I'd done a thorough cleaning just yesterday in hopes that Christina would come home with me tonight. Those plans had been wrecked by Jade.

Keeping my distance, I unlocked my door and gestured for her to enter first. As she walked past me, I caught a whiff of her perfume; it was stronger than usual, almost cloying. She'd clearly dressed for what she'd hoped would be a very different kind of evening. If I wasn't so angry about her intrusion and rudeness towards Christina, I would have felt guilty over how coldly I was treating her, but I felt she had crossed a line by showing up.

"Let's find this sketchbook and get you on your way," I said firmly. "I have somewhere I need to be."

Jade turned to face me, her head tilted slightly. "Yes, I'm sure you do." Her smile was sharp enough to cut glass. "With that stuck-up BMW bitch."

The way she spoke about Christina made the hair on the back of my neck stand.

Her stiff body relaxed, and her demeanor shifted. She smiled at me. "I'm still willing, if you are," she said, running her finger down her loose blouse, then nodding her head towards the bedroom.

"I don't think that's a good idea, Jade."

Her body again stiffened. "Fine, Jesus. You're so uptight. I thought this was all fun and casual. Why do you care who fucks you tonight? I'll leave you spent. You know it. Prissy BMW girl is probably a bad lay."

It was a side of Jade I hadn't seen until that night. And I didn't like it.

"Please. Just grab what you need and go. We'll talk later."

Jade scoffed as she turned around abruptly and walked into my bedroom. I peered inside and she seemed to be checking out the bed. Did she like seeing that it was made? That she had thrown cold water on my night with Christina?

She went into the bathroom. I moved, more out of curiosity as to where she'd left her sketchbook since I hadn't seen it. But before I could follow her, she came out waving the sketchbook at me.

"Got it," she said, walking out of my bedroom.

"Where was it?"

She ignored my question. "Well, since you don't want me, I guess I'll go."

I nodded. "Thank you." I didn't know what else to

say. I just wanted to diffuse the awkwardness and get her to leave so I could jump in my car, put the pedal to the metal and get to Christina's house.

Jade stormed off angrily. I watched from my window and saw get into her car and drive off. I grabbed my jacket and keys and ran out of my apartment as I texted Christina.

"On my way."

She texted back a smiling wink emoji.

NINE
ETHAN

Within minutes of Jade leaving, I was out the door and in my SUV. I made the ten-minute drive to Christina's house in five minutes.

She had been waiting for me, leaning against her front door with a knowing smile.

We picked right up where we had left off in my apartment.

Christina wasn't as wild as Jade.

She didn't take control with the same reckless abandon. But she was a warm, giving, generous lover.

Her touch was softer, slower, more in line with what I'd known before Jade.

I felt more comfortable making love to Christina. Like I wasn't out of my element, playing a part in a *9-1/2 Weeks*-like movie with Jade.

That night, as we lay tangled in the sheets, her

breath warm against my chest, I felt a sense of peace I hadn't realized I'd been missing with Jade.

For the next two weeks, it was all Christina.

She worked closer to my place than her house, so it quickly became routine for her to stay over. It made sense—easier than driving all the way to Whitlock late at night, only to turn around and come back to Fairdale for work in the morning.

It was convenient. And I didn't mind. I enjoyed having her around.

It wasn't like she'd moved in. She didn't stay every night. It didn't feel serious—at least, not in that way. Not yet.

But close enough that I knew the way she liked her coffee—black, no sugar, always in a to-go mug.

Enough that I had to clear out a drawer for her clothes so she didn't have to keep bringing an overnight bag.

Enough that I started getting used to waking up next to her.

Jade was upset.

Jade: *So this is it? You're just done with me?*

Ethan: *Jade, it was always casual. That hasn't changed.*

Jade: *Oh, right. Casual. Are you casual with her too?*

Ethan: *Matter of a fact, I am. I've been upfront.*

Jade: *Well, lally la la. Good for you.*

Then, just as suddenly as she had been upset, she changed her tune. Maybe the time apart made her realize what we'd had was not a serious relationship but a fun fling. And she had finally gotten over me.

Jade: *Hey, I'm sorry about how I've been acting lately. I shouldn't have dropped by that night. It was weird. Won't happen again.*

Ethan: *I appreciate that.*

Jade: *I meant it when I said I'm fine with things being casual. I just... let my emotions get the best of me for a second. Won't happen again. Can we stay friends?*

Ethan: *Yeah, I'd like that.*

And that was that.

At least, it seemed like it was.

With Jade out of the picture, my life settled into something resembling normal again.

One thing I had been adamant about since my divorce was that Tyler didn't meet the women I dated. I didn't want him getting attached to someone who would not be around long term. But when Christina invited me to a BBQ at her place—and mentioned her son, Robbie, would be there—I hesitated.

Was this a step too far? Was I committing to something more by agreeing to this? There I went again, overthinking things. It wasn't like we were introducing them as anything more than kids hanging out while the adults had a beer and a burger on a nice summer day.

I felt different about Christina. I could see getting more serious with her than I had been with Jade.

So I agreed.

Tyler wasn't thrilled. From the moment we pulled into Christina's driveway, he eyed me with suspicion.

"Who is she?" he asked, arms crossed.

I kept my tone casual. "A friend."

"A girlfriend?" he said, sounding upset.

"No, it's not like that. Christina and I are just friends. That's it."

"Does Mom know?"

I suppressed a laugh. "Of course. It's no big deal, buddy."

He still eyed me suspiciously, but that seemed to satisfy him—at least for now.

Tyler and Robbie, who was a year older, seemed to get along fine in an awkward, boyish way; they just ran around and occasionally acknowledged each other's presence. They then bonded over video games. Even though it was a beautiful day outside, the boys were tethered to the large monitor of a computer, each boy holding game controllers tightly. I recognized the game Mario Kart, which both Kayla and I allowed him to play, so I let him be. It was nice for Christina and me to spend some time alone outdoors. We drank cold beers, ate cheeseburgers and potato salad, and relaxed in her backyard.

It felt... easy.

Comfortable.

Like something that could last.

Which made me nervous and confused. And I kept thinking about Kayla. We were divorced, so why did I care what she would think?

When I dropped Tyler off at Kayla's later that night, she greeted me with her usual raised eyebrow of suspicion.

"So... you and Christina, huh?"

I sighed. "Tyler already told you?"

She smirked. "Of course he did. You think he's not reporting back? Looks like you two are getting serious."

I waved her off. "No, we're just dating. It's non-exclusive."

Kayla nodded, but there was something in her expression that said she wasn't fully buying it.

"I mean, it's none of my business," she said, leaning against the doorframe, "but you know... now that she's around Tyler, my mom-spidey sense goes up."

I understood. If the roles were reversed, I'd absolutely be concerned about a new man entering Tyler's life. And I had no clue if Kayla had been dating—I assumed she had. She had needs, just like I did. She was a beautiful woman with big black eyes and olive skin, and I was sure she got asked on dates all the time.

We had been divorced for fifteen months now. I highly doubted she had gone without sex that long, even if it was just a quick hookup kind of thing. I'd even tried searching for her on Vibing, wondering if she was there, but I never came across her profile.

The curiosity got the best of me.

"So, are you seeing anyone?"

Kayla laughed a little too quickly. "No." Then she paused. "And I really don't feel comfortable talking about our dating lives."

I chuckled. "Fair enough."

She was right. This all felt a little strange.

TEN
JADE

I wasn't the kind of woman who got jealous. At least, that's what I had always told myself.

Ethan was clear from the start; he wasn't interested in a serious relationship, only in casual dating, which in man-speak meant casual sex.

He just wanted a girl to hook up with for guilt-free sex without strings attached. So I went into this with both eyes wide open. But let's be honest: There is no such thing as that when it comes to a sexual relationship. I had been trying to make it work—but then Ethan completely shut me out of his life. I told him I was fine with the status quo of just having fun. Yet even that now was no longer an option. And I missed him. There went the no-strings-attached theory out the window.

I wasn't used to being turned down when throwing

myself into a man's bed like I had done with Ethan, regardless of our relationship status.

And now I felt down on myself. Ethan's rejection. The humiliation of going to his apartment unannounced only to find that he was on a date with another woman. I'd just made things worse by not leaving, but I was curious as to what this new girl looked like.

It was hard for me to admit, but I seemed to be a magnet for bad relationships.

I'm not proud of having slept with a few married men in my life. I didn't know one was married until way later, so I didn't feel guilty about that affair. He was just a dirtbag cheating lout for lying about it.

The others, I was guilty as charged. I knew I was the other woman going in.

It was thrilling at first, but then the baggage and destruction those affairs eventually unleashed were too much to bear, so I stopped.

It's why I now preferred to stick to the dating apps. I'm not naïve. I know there are married men on the apps who are pretending to be single when they're not. A lot of men are pigs. But I knew right away Ethan was the real deal. And I understood why he didn't want to jump into a serious relationship, having been divorced for barely a year.

Ethan never agreed to exclusivity, so why did I feel like I had been cheated on? It didn't help that she was prettier, thinner than I was. And she drove a luxury car. I felt like a gnat that night.

So I tried to focus on how things began for Ethan and me.

The beginning of a sexual relationship, exploring each other's bodies for the first time, was always so thrilling and intoxicating. Seeing what makes the other squirm in ecstasy.

I was four years older than Ethan, and I liked that. I felt like a cougar. Like in the movies. *Are you trying to seduce me, Mrs. Robinson?*

We had been going at it like a couple of wild banshees in heat. Even doing it in our vehicles, and out in the woods. We were going hot and heavy until he put the brakes on our fling. And I won't lie, it hurt. But I respected his wishes. At least, I tried. And yet, there I was, standing outside Ethan's apartment complex that night like a desperate lovesick idiot, waiting for him to let me in—when it was obvious he didn't want me anywhere near him that night.

The moment I saw her, I wanted to disappear.

Ethan had that look on his face. The one men get when they're so into a woman that they don't even see anyone else in the room. I never saw that look towards me. He looked at me with lust, but not like he looked at her, with longing. That probably hurt the most.

For the first few days after that awful night outside of Ethan's apartment, I wanted to text him. To apologize. To see if there was still a chance. But my pride wouldn't let me. I had already humiliated myself once. I wasn't about to do it again. So, instead, I ignored him.

And when he didn't reach out, I knew.

He had moved on.

At first, I was furious. Not just at him, but at myself for letting some other woman take up space in my head. I wasn't that girl. I didn't sit around crying over men.

So I made myself busy. Luckily, I had the perfect distraction. A house flip in Eureka, about fifty miles north of Fairdale. It was a rundown two-bedroom bungalow, nothing fancy, but it had good bones.

I spent long hours with my crew of construction workers fixing it up, throwing myself into the job. Tearing up old carpet. Painting. Fixing drywall. Manual labor had a way of exhausting my body just enough to shut my brain off at night.

And for a while, it worked.

I didn't think about Ethan. I stopped wondering if he was spending nights with Christina the way he used to with me.

And then, after about a week, I felt... fine.

I told myself I was over it. I even texted Ethan to prove it to myself.

Jade: *Hey, I'm sorry for how I acted. I shouldn't have dropped by that night. It was weird. Won't happen again.*

Ethan: *I appreciate that.*

Jade: *I meant it when I said I'm fine with things*

being casual. I just... let my emotions get the best of me for a second. Won't happen again. Can we stay friends?

Ethan: *Yeah, I'd like that.*

And that was it.

I told myself it was closure.

I even started dating again—a few matches on Vibing, a few dinner dates. Didn't make any meaningful connections like I had with Ethan, but it was fun. But when my phone buzzed, I still hoped it was Ethan. It never was. It was once more obvious he had moved on.

When I worked late at the house in Eureka, I still thought about texting him, asking if he wanted to grab a drink at Bigfoot's.

But I left it alone. I left *him* alone.

My phone buzzed. I looked at it, hoping it was Ethan, but it wasn't. It was a one-word text message from an unknown number.

WHORE.

ELEVEN
ETHAN

I SPENT THE NIGHT AT CHRISTINA'S HOUSE. IT WAS only the third time since she usually preferred staying at my apartment—it was so much closer to her work compared to her place.

Robbie had spent the night with Christina's mom, Dana. I had only met Dana once. She seemed nice enough, though perhaps a little wary or standoffish, but I supposed that was normal when meeting the guy your daughter was dating. I had a sneaking suspicion Christina had shared details about our non-exclusive arrangement. Dana probably saw me as some commitment-phobic jerk messing around with her daughter's emotions. I couldn't exactly blame her for being cold towards me.

. . .

The next morning, I found myself in Christina's bathroom, preparing to head back to Fairdale. Like the rest of her house, the bathroom was spotless—white subway tiles, a sleek marble vanity, the pristine glass shower doors free of water spots. Everything was arranged with such precise neatness, it almost felt staged, like something from a magazine shoot.

Usually, I used the guest bathroom down the hallway, but Christina told me to just use the en suite bathroom. It was more convenient, so I grabbed my shave kit and took care of business as she headed to the kitchen to make coffee.

After using the toilet, I washed up and brushed my teeth. When brushing my hair, I noticed the mirror was one of those with a medicine cabinet built in. *Don't even think about it,* I told myself, but it was too late. I'd never been the type to snoop, so why was it so compelling to do just that?

I had never riffled through a woman's things, never searched Kayla's phone or purse during our marriage. I had friends who bragged about doing exactly that, and I always found it deeply unsettling. If trust had deteriorated to the point that you felt compelled to go through a woman's things behind her back, maybe it was time to call it quits on that relationship. And yet... There I stood, running the brush through my hair needlessly one more time.

I glanced back toward the bathroom door, ears straining to pick up any sign of Christina approaching.

She was still in the kitchen, humming softly, the distant clink of coffee mugs reassuring me she wasn't heading this way.

I knew I shouldn't. But curiosity tugged at me like an itch I couldn't reach. Maybe it was how carefully everything was arranged. I imagined the inside of the medicine cabinet would be neatly organized, or perhaps it was just my nagging sense that despite how much time we'd spent together, Christina remained oddly elusive about herself.

Before my better judgment could intervene, I reached up and cracked the cabinet open—just an inch, then another. I felt like a thief, glancing nervously over my shoulder again, absurdly imagining her bursting in and catching me in the act.

As I suspected, inside everything was lined up with meticulous precision. A sleek electric toothbrush, a bright pink razor, a small glass bottle of perfume labeled with some French name I couldn't pronounce. Bottles of moisturizers and expensive-looking serums, neatly arranged by size and shape. After years married to Kayla, I'd grown used to these things, even appreciating them; she'd even gotten me into a care routine for my dry skin issues.

What are you doing? I chided myself as I closed the door, but then something caught my eye. I didn't close the door; instead I leaned in closer, my eyes drawn to a small prescription bottle sitting next to a bottle of Advil.

The orange prescription bottle sat innocently in place, fitting seamlessly into the perfect alignment of her cabinet. But a prescription on the label jumped out at me: Lithium.

I knew exactly what lithium was prescribed for. The word echoed in my mind, a stark memory from my past.

My older sister, Natalie, had struggled with mental health problems most of her adult life. She had been diagnosed as bipolar and had been prescribed lithium to treat the disorder, specifically to manage manic episodes and prevent recurrences of both manic and depressive episodes.

My heart sped up slightly, anxiety gnawing at the edges of my thoughts. The urge to pick up the bottle and examine it closely surged through me. I wanted to see the dosage, the prescribing doctor's name, how many pills remained. I wanted confirmation of something, though I wasn't entirely sure what, so I reached for it—but right away, I clenched my fist and pulled my hand away. *What am I doing?* I had no right.

I swallowed hard and closed the medicine cabinet door with exaggerated care, making sure it wasn't too loud and that I was leaving it exactly how I'd found it. But the unease lingered, twisting and coiling in my gut.

It didn't have to mean anything, right?

Plenty of people like my sister took lithium to manage mood disorders effectively every day. It had brought stability to my sister's chaotic ups and downs.

Because of what she had gone through, I knew about the stigma of mental illness—how unfair, how misguided it was. If you have a headache, you take something for it. If you have high blood pressure, you take something for it. This was no different. I hated myself for the judgment I'd felt rising within me when I saw lithium in her medicine cabinet.

Yet the thought continued looping stubbornly through my head.

The prescription seemed to be working well for Christina. She was so put together, so composed, so effortlessly confident. Not at all like Natalie had been. My sister had struggled continuously, veering wildly from manic energy to crushing depression, cycling through doctors, medications, and hospitals. She had never found stability, no matter how hard she tried.

I should be praising her for taking care of her mental health. So why did it unsettle me so much?

I exhaled slowly, steadying myself. *This doesn't mean anything.*

So why couldn't I shake the nagging discomfort about my discovery?

Forcing the intrusive thoughts down, I wiped my hands thoroughly, determined to act casual, as if I hadn't just violated Christina's privacy and uncovered something unsettling. God, what was wrong with me?

I stepped out of the bathroom, putting on a carefree expression as I walked into the kitchen.

Christina turned, her face brightening as she poured fresh coffee into two mugs. "Everything okay?"

I nodded, probably a little too quickly. "Yeah. All good."

She handed me the mug, her fingertips grazing mine gently. "Cream and sugar are on the counter if you need them."

"Thank you," I said, taking a careful sip, watching her quietly over the rim of the mug.

Christina looked exactly the same as always—bright, calm, entirely in control.

"We're good, right?" I asked. I don't know why I asked her that. But I had been feeling guilty that perhaps I was sending her mixed messages like I had to Jade since we had spent a lot of time together. We hadn't had a discussion about where we stood in our relationship for a while. I suppose seeing the lithium in her medicine cabinet made me uneasy. The last thing I wanted was to be the spark plug in a mental health crisis.

She looked at me strangely. "Yeah, of course. Why are you asking?"

I shrugged. "We've been spending a lot of time together lately, so just wanted to make sure you were okay with what we have."

"It's all good, don't worry."

She smiled, leaned in and kissed me.

I wanted to believe her.

TWELVE
ETHAN

I WAS AT WORK THE NEXT DAY WHEN MY PHONE buzzed. It was a text from Christina which made me expect one of the usual light-hearted, flirty messages she would send while we were both stuck at our jobs. I pulled up the text to read it and could feel the smile leaving my face. I froze, staring at the message she'd sent me.

I think we should move in together.

I finally blinked and re-read it again. What? I was confused. We had just talked about this yesterday, and she had reassured me that we were on the same page. Where was this coming from suddenly, and via text?

For a minute, I thought about it. She had to be messing with me. A joke. A prank. Maybe she thought she was being funny. But I wasn't laughing.

I typed out a response, keeping it light; I didn't

want to overreact. *We just talked about this yesterday. I like keeping things how they are. You agreed.*

Waiting for her to reply, I stared at my phone. The three dots appeared right away, bubbling on the screen. Then they disappeared. Came back. And disappeared again.

I could almost see her hesitating, rewording her thoughts, debating what to say next. I couldn't look away. I held my phone and my eyes bored into the screen.

Christina was a confident woman. Direct. She didn't play coy, didn't beat around the bush. But this? This felt different. I liked her. A lot. What we had could have blossomed into something more than casual dating. Yet I wasn't ready to take our relationship to that level. We'd only been dating for a month. Had never discussed or even hinted at cohabitating. And it was certainly not something to talk about over a text message.

There was zero chance I was making a decision that impacted not just me but Tyler over a seven-word text message. She had to be joking. So I didn't freak out. Waited for her to reply with a 'gotcha' message.

Finally, she replied, and it wasn't playful. It wasn't, *I was joking around*. Far from it.

Christina: *Don't you love me? I love you!*

I put the phone down like it was burning my hands. What was she doing? We hadn't said that to each other in real life. Never even come close to having that conversation. Now, in the span of a few minutes and two text messages, she had told me that she wanted us to live together and that she loved me. Over text. Who does that? I felt like I had stepped into some alternate version of our relationship.

Where was this coming from?

I took a deep breath, knowing I had to shut this down and just be honest.

If I hadn't been at work, I would have called her. But I didn't want to get into an emotionally charged phone discussion or, even worse, an argument while sitting at my desk. So I began to type a reply telling myself to keep it simple and clear. Polite but firm. Convincing myself I wasn't in the wrong. At the very least, we should discuss this in person, but she hadn't given me that option. I typed my message.

Ethan: *I'm sorry, but I don't feel that way. I like you a lot. But I've been very honest with you from the start that I wasn't looking for a serious relationship. That hasn't changed. I'm still only interested in casual dating. Non-exclusive. And we should have discussed it in person, not over text.*

I hit send. I watched it go out into the ether, my heart thumping. I watched the message be delivered. Then an acknowledgment that it was read, which made my heart beat even harder.

I waited for a couple of minutes. No reply.

Ten minutes passed. Nothing.

Then, finally, after around twenty minutes, her reply arrived.

Christina: *You have ruined my life. I hate you and never want to see you again.*

I read her message, dumbfounded. Had I been too harsh? I rubbed a hand over my face. My head throbbed.

I figured she would be upset, but this felt over the top.

I debated if I should just stop corresponding, but I felt bad at how terribly things were ending between us, so I exhaled and typed a final message.

Ethan: *I'm sorry you feel that way. I didn't want to hurt you. I won't message you again.*

Hurting her was the last thing I wanted to do. Just yesterday, she was happy and fine. I suppose she was hiding her true feelings, and I was too obtuse to see it. But she had ended our fling and didn't want to hear from me again. I would respect that.

Still processing what had happened, I received another message from Christina. I hoped she would understand and we could at least end on a more positive note, but I was wrong. Way wrong. I couldn't believe what she had just texted back.

Fuck you. Limp dick asshole.

I stared at the screen, my entire body tensing. That escalated fast, I thought.

I didn't know what had just happened, but I was

done. So I tried to shake it off and focus on work, but I couldn't.

One of my coworkers noticed I was suddenly a bit off.

"You good, man?" Jeff, the guy in the cubicle next to me, asked me when we saw me heading towards the bathroom.

"Yeah, just tired," I muttered.

I didn't need to tell anyone at work that my casual hookup had just flipped a switch and declared me the ruin of her existence.

Although I wanted to reach out to end things on better terms, I decided that wasn't wise; it was best to put the exchange behind me. I wouldn't bother Christina again. But it hurt that things had ended like this—so bitter, so ugly. So out of the blue.

Then, an hour later, my phone buzzed. It was Christina.

I hesitated. Maybe she had calmed down. Maybe she was reaching out to apologize. So I pulled up the message. It wasn't an apology.

You're a piece of shit. You came into my life, turned it upside down, and now you just walk away without a care in the world. You selfish prick.

I sighed and didn't respond. Then she sent another message.

Then another.

And another.

Each was worse than the last. Vile. Vicious. Explosive. A side to Christina that I hadn't seen before. Not even an inkling that she could be so nasty.

I silenced my phone, placed it face-down on my desk, and kept my hands off it for the rest of the workday.

As I was wrapping up my day at work, I decided to check my phone and I couldn't believe what I saw. She hadn't stopped sending me nasty text messages all day long. She had sent thirty-two messages in about ninety minutes.

I swallowed hard, scrolling through them.

Every single one was an unhinged, blithering attack.

You ruined my life.

I hate you.

You're a pathetic excuse for a man.

You're a lousy lay.

Faked every orgasm, stupid.

Rot in hell.

I got angry. What the hell was her problem? This wasn't just angst over a breakup she'd started—it was a full-on meltdown.

The moment 5:00 p.m. hit, I grabbed my stuff and walked out the door.

I sat in my car, hesitating before unlocking my phone to read the messages. The message count had climbed now to fifty-one. And eleven missed calls.

Quickly, I scrolled through them, skimming for anything remotely rational.

But there was none of that, just pure venom directed at me.

Even while driving home, my phone buzzed nonstop. Every few seconds, another message. Another insult. One after the other.

I STOLE a glance at the screen as I drove. It was still Christina blowing up my phone with nasty messages. What had happened to the easygoing, chill, adorable woman I had been seeing just twenty-fours ago?

Gritting my teeth, I gripped the wheel. One would think we can just ignore this type of abuse. Wait it out. But the relentless pace of these vitriolic messages began to wear me down mentally. I thought about Christina's state of mental health. Something had to be wrong with her. People just don't act this way.

Then my mind flashed to the medicine cabinet and the plastic orange container of prescription pills. The lithium.

Was this... was this some kind of mental breakdown? A manic episode? I wasn't a mental health expert, but that could explain her actions.

This wasn't just a bad breakup reaction. This was something else.

Something worse.

By the time I pulled into my apartment's parking lot, I couldn't help but wonder what else she was capable of doing. How dark would this get? I was worried about what she might do or say to get back at me, but I also worried about her. I couldn't help it.

Beyond the amount of abuse she was hurling my way, I feared that she might do something to harm herself. I felt like reaching out to make sure she wouldn't go down roads of no return, but I decided against it. I didn't want to upset her even more than she was already. I wouldn't reply to any of it; she had to get tired of sending all these messages. How long could she keep this up?

THIRTEEN
ETHAN

Over the next few days, things didn't get better. In fact, they got much worse.

My phone became a portal to Christina's increasingly unhinged mind.

Each time it buzzed, my pulse quickened and anxiety tightened in my chest. Her messages were relentless and disturbingly aggressive. I tried to ignore them, hoping she'd eventually tire herself out and stop. But ignoring her seemed to have the opposite effect, seemingly making her more upset.

Ignoring me won't work, asshole.

You think you can blow up my life and just walk away scot-free? Think again!

I scrolled through one message after another, my stomach churning at the twisted words she spewed.

You're a coward, Ethan. A spineless coward who

thinks it's okay to take advantage of someone and just walk away.

You think you're safe? Think again. You don't get to ruin lives without consequences.

Her words grew increasingly threatening, darkening more at each new text. I knew I had to do something to stop this madness. I considered reporting her to the police, but I wanted to get her to stop on her own without getting her in trouble with the cops. But I had to do something. I couldn't go on like this.

Finally, unable to handle another assault of vile messages, I typed out a reply, trying to keep my hands steady. I didn't want to insult her or be mean spirited, though I wanted to yell at her, *Knock it the fuck off, psycho.* But that wouldn't work. I wasn't going to get down into the mud with her So I tried to be even keeled in my text message: *Christina, you need to stop. Seriously. Leave me alone. What you're doing is harassment, and it's not okay. Please get some professional help for your obvious mental health issues. I've moved on, and you need to as well. Let's be adults about this and go our separate ways.*

I hesitated briefly, hovering over the send button. I knew this might escalate things further, but maybe it would finally shock her into realizing how out of control she'd become. Perhaps she was enraged, so hurt that she didn't even realize she had sent me over one hundred nasty text messages in just a few days. I hit send.

Her reply came almost immediately. Her anger burst forth in a furious torrent of text messages.

How dare you question my mental health? You're the one who's fucked up, Ethan. You're too scared, too pathetic, to commit to a real woman like me. No wonder your marriage failed. Kayla must have known you were worthless.

And then, her rage shifted its target to Jade. The mention of Jade made my blood run cold. How did she know her name? Aside from that awkward brief encounter outside of my apartment when Jade crashed our first date, Christina and Jade didn't know each other. I sure as hell hadn't introduced them that night. And as far as I knew, they hadn't met each other since then. I'd talked to Christina about Kayla, but not about Vibing casual dates.

Christina wrote: *You went back to your fat slut Jade, didn't you? She's nothing but a disgusting, cocksucking whore. How desperate do you have to be to crawl back into bed with that pathetic slug?*

It didn't seem possible, but each new message grew more vicious, more disgusting. Her language turned more and more vile, dripping with hate and venom, making my skin crawl. The insults were crude, personal, and deeply unsettling.

I hope your fat whore gives you an STD and your limp dick falls off, Ethan. You don't deserve happiness. You deserve pain.

I couldn't handle it anymore. Enough was enough.

Taking a deep breath, I blocked her number. The moment the confirmation appeared on my screen, I felt a fleeting sense of relief. I should have done this right away. Surely, now the nightmare would end.

But the peace was short-lived.

When I checked my email later that day, my stomach twisted again. Thirty new emails filled my inbox, every single one from Christina. I clicked on the first, my heart pounding hard against my rib cage.

I didn't think it was possible, but the emails were worse than the text messages.

Each one was lengthy, filled with thousands of manic words. One email overflowed with love and devotion, pleading for forgiveness, promising we could start afresh. The very next descended back into madness, filled with disgusting insults, wild accusations, and hateful rants.

You are my soulmate, Ethan. I can't live without you. Why don't you see that?

I'll never forgive you for destroying my life. You're a monster, Ethan. A disgusting, selfish monster who deserves every misery life has in store for you.

The erratic swings between love and hatred terrified me. It was as though two entirely different personalities were fighting for control of her mind.

I blocked her email address as well, trying to calm the frantic pounding in my chest. That had to be the end of it, I reassured myself.

My phone buzzed again. I retrieved it, my stomach

sinking as I saw multiple notifications from unknown numbers.

You think blocking me will save you? You're pathetic.

You're not a real man!

The threats escalated, now coming from a multitude of anonymous numbers. Random email addresses began flooding my inbox, all clearly from Christina, mocking my attempts to block her.

What did I tell you, idiot? You can't block me. You can't erase me like I'm nothing.

You chose this, Ethan. You chose this when you broke me. There are consequences. Severe consequences.

I slumped back, numb with shock. Dread twisted in my gut.

Ignoring her wasn't working. Blocking her was futile. She had found a way around every obstacle I'd set up. I felt trapped, cornered. I started pacing around my apartment, running my fingers through my hair. What else could I possibly do to make this stop?

Calling the police once again flashed through my mind, but I quickly dismissed the idea. The thought of Christina going through the humiliation and trauma of being arrested or questioned by the authorities was something I wasn't ready to bear. Despite everything, I felt sorry for her. Clearly, she wasn't well. But sympathy wouldn't keep me safe.

I had no one to turn to. How could I explain this to

Kayla or my friends without them judging me or, worse, thinking I had somehow provoked Christina into this spiral? A womanizing lout getting what he deserved.

I stared at my phone, dreading every new vibration, every ping signaling another venomous message. Each notification felt like a tightening noose, suffocating and relentless. I couldn't escape, trapped in a cage Christina had built, bar by bar, message by message. Just looking at my phone made me feel anxious, like a panic attack was coming on.

Another notification. This one was different.

My heart seized as I opened the message. It wasn't just a text. This time, she'd sent a photograph. My blood ran cold, a chill crawling up my spine.

It was a photograph of Jade's house with an ominous message: *You can't have your happily ever after with that slut.*

Her next message came in:

You'll wish you never met me, Ethan. I promise you that.

I wanted to text her back: *Oh, don't worry, I already wish that.* But there was no sense in poking an angry bear.

FOURTEEN
ETHAN

THE PHOTOGRAPH OF JADE'S HOUSE HAUNTED ME. I stared at my phone screen, my hands trembling slightly. Christina had gone from obsessive and angry to dangerously unpredictable. As far as I could tell, this wasn't just harassment anymore—it had become a direct threat against Jade.

Christina had somehow got it in her head that I was seeing Jade again, and that wasn't even true.

Anxiety churned my stomach, doubling me in pain. It was bad enough to harass me, but why bring Jade into this? I hadn't spoken to her in over a month. Hadn't even thought much about her beyond casual curiosity, wondering how she was doing. Smiling at the memories of our lovemaking.

Yet Christina was fixated, convinced Jade was the reason I had ended things between us. I needed to call

Jade and warn her about the crazy woman out there. God, this was so embarrassing.

I jumped when my phone buzzed again, fearing it was another nasty threat from Christina. To my relief, it wasn't Christina but Jade. I read the message.

Hey Ethan. Can we talk? Something weird is going on.

Oh, God, was Christina sending Jade nasty messages too? I called her, and she picked up right away.

"Hey," she answered, her voice tight.

"Are you okay?" I asked, trying to sound calm despite the hammering in my chest.

She exhaled heavily. "Not really. Someone keyed my car. It's pretty bad—deep scratches all over. And right before that, I got some nasty texts."

I shut my eyes, pinching the bridge of my nose. "From who?" I knew the answer.

"I-I don't know. An unknown number sent them. But they seem to know me. And you."

"What did they say?"

She hesitated, then sighed. "They're calling me names. Saying horrible things about me. And saying weird stuff about you—about us. There's not even an 'us' anymore, but they sure think we're still seeing each other." Her voice trailed off. I could hear her trying to hold back from crying. "Do you know who this is? What's going on, Ethan?"

"Yeah, I know who that is," I admitted reluctantly.

"Her name is Christina Garza. I met her through the dating app. We'd been going out for a month. But I broke it off with her a few days ago and she became very upset. She's been harassing me for days now. Sending horrible messages and threats. I'm really sorry, Jade. I never thought she'd drag you into this."

There was a long silence on the other end of the line. "Christina? That's the woman from your apartment, right?"

"Yes. And she's not okay. I did not know she would react like this."

"Did you tell her about me? About us?"

"No, I swear. I don't know how she figured out your name or where you live to mess with your car. I'm so sorry. How bad is the damage?"

Jade's voice trembled. "It's bad. These are long and deep scratches that won't buff out."

Christina's crazy, I thought.

"I'm coming over," I said firmly. "I'll be there in ten minutes."

When I arrived at Jade's house, she was waiting outside for me, sitting on the top step of her front stoop. Although she had a pained expression on her face, she gave me a wan smile when she saw me.

Seeing her again sent a pang through me. I hadn't realized how much I'd missed her; missed her amiable smile, her humor, her effortless way of putting me at ease. But now her expression was clouded by worry and frustration.

"Hey," I said, approaching cautiously. I didn't know if she was pissed off at me for getting her mixed up in this mess.

"Hi. It's good to see you again, despite the circumstances," she said, gesturing towards her car parked in her driveway.

"It is nice to see you, Jade," I said, surprised by how much I meant it. I gave her a hug, which she accepted as she hugged me back tightly. I then turned my attention to her car.

The gouged metal glared in the sunlight. Deep angry scars across the paint.

"I'm so sorry, Jade. This is all my fault."

She shook her head. "You can't blame yourself for someone else's crazy actions." But her eyes were sad, wary, and I hated myself for being the reason behind that look. Because there wasn't any doubt: If it weren't for me, Christina wouldn't have done that to Jade's car.

We walked closer to survey the deep, deliberate scratches etched violently across the car's surface. I ran my hand over the marks, feeling sick to my stomach. Christina must have used a knife or a large flathead screwdriver to leave that type of damage; this wasn't an old-fashioned key job. I thought I had seen Christina's darkest side from her messages, but despite the hell she had put me through these past few days, I didn't think she would actually take it to this level. To go from words to an actual physical act of vandalism.

"Have you contacted the police?" I asked gently.

Jade shook her head. "Not yet. Honestly, I wasn't sure what to do. I thought maybe it was a random asshole until the messages came."

"Can I see them?" She handed me her phone. There was a string of text messages from a blocked number. The messages were sent as if in a frenzy, like Christina had done to me as well.

You are a whore who should have stayed away from Ethan.

Slut

Get our own man, bitch

Beelzebub

Stay away from Ethan or it gets worse, slut!

I couldn't believe this was happening. I didn't even know what to say.

"I'm sorry about all this," I said barely above a whisper.

She paused, looking at me with uncertainty. "I should report this to the police, shouldn't I?"

"I don't know," I admitted, conflicted. "I don't want things to escalate even more. But this is crossing a line."

"You're damn right. Look at my car, Ethan. Do you think she might get physical... with me?" she asked, trembling.

I reached for her and held her in a tight embrace. "I won't let anything happen to you." I didn't know what compelled me to say that. I just wanted to comfort her, to make her feel safe.

We stood there in her driveway, embracing silently

for a moment. Jade glanced sideways at me. "Come inside for a bit. We can talk about it more."

In her kitchen, Jade brewed coffee while I sat nervously at the table, my leg bouncing. I didn't think I would be back at her place—especially not under these dire circumstances. I could see her hands shaking slightly as she put down two mugs.

"So sorry she dragged you into this," I repeated. "I never thought I would get caught up in my mess. I'll pay for the damage to your car."

Jade's expression softened, and she reached across the table, caressing my hand. "I already told you. It's not your fault. No matter what happened between you two, there is no excuse to do crazy shit like this." She held up her phone, showing me a picture of her damaged car. She then leaned in and placed her hand gently on my shoulder. "Don't worry about the car. That's why I have insurance. Let them pay for the damage, not you." She smiled at me.

Her touch comforted me more than it should have. It was over a month since I'd last seen her, yet her presence immediately soothed some of the tension that had lodged deep in my chest these past few days.

I asked Jade if she had security cameras covering her driveway, as it would be great to have a nice crisp video of Christina damaging Jade's car in our arsenal against her. Perhaps with that type of hard evidence, we could get her to stop and leave us alone. To my disappointment, Jade said she didn't have security cameras. Not even a Ring doorbell, considering nothing bad ever happened in sleepy Fairdale.

"So if you don't want to get the police involved, what should we do?" she asked quietly, sipping her coffee. "I mean, what are you going to do? Do you think she'll actually stop if we ignore her?"

"I don't know," I confessed, rubbing my face wearily. "Ignoring and blocking her made things worse. She's sending messages from different numbers now. I've blocked her emails, but she just creates new accounts. It's like an obsession."

Jade's brows knit together. "I'm scared, Ethan. What if she does to me what she did to my car? She could kill me."

A wave of helplessness washed over me.

"I didn't want to ruin her life even more by involving authorities, but now she's targeted you. And gotten physical. We might not have a choice in the matter anymore when it comes to getting the cops involved."

Her expression was thoughtful, Jade sat back. "Maybe we wait. Give it a few more days. She might burn out and leave us alone."

"I thought the same thing," I said quietly. "But now I'm not so sure."

We sat in anxious silence. Jade's eyes flicked to her damaged car outside, her shoulders slumping slightly. She gave me a weak smile, but her eyes reflected my own doubts. We sat in silence, neither of us truly believing my promise of safety.

Then Jade stood up. She leaned in. I thought she was going for my empty coffee cup to take it to the kitchen, but she kissed me. I kissed her back, and it felt nice. Like it had been before. Before I let Christina into my life.

As I LEFT Jade's house a while later, I glanced around nervously, paranoia creeping in. I could feel Christina's presence, her anger hovering unseen in the shadows out there somewhere. I was terrified that she'd seen me visiting Jade, and I shuddered at what she might do next. How far was Christina capable of going? But I shook that thought off. She was not an ever-present boogeyman.

I got into my jeep and started the engine. My phone buzzed. A new text message. I read it.

The message was short, chilling, and though it was from a blocked caller, it was unmistakably Christina's.

Did you have a pleasant visit with your whore? You think Jade's car looks bad? Just wait until you see what happens next to that slut.

FIFTEEN
ETHAN

It was Saturday morning. Tyler was spending the weekend with me. I was trying not to let him know what was going on, trying hard to seem *normal*. I made us a hearty breakfast of scrambled eggs, crispy bacon, and toast. Big glasses of freshly squeezed orange juice.

The time spent making breakfast and scarfing down the meal with Tyler was a welcome distraction.

After we were done with breakfast, Tyler asked if he could play a video game with his friends. I said sure, but he would not spend all day in my tiny apartment. He said, "Sure, Dad" as he ran off into his bedroom.

A hard yawn reminded me I'd hardly gotten any sleep last night. Just wound up walking around my bedroom and around the living room. I found myself constantly looking out my windows, certain that Christina was out there in the dark watching me. God, was this what paranoia was like? Why would coke sniffers do this to themselves?

I was as clueless about what to do with Christina as when I went to bed, which made me feel frustrated and helpless.

A knock on the door jolted me from my restless pacing. My heart skipped a beat, anxiety spiking immediately. I wasn't expecting anyone. And whoever was standing outside my door knocking had bypassed the front-entrance security door. Wasn't the first time someone made it inside without buzzing; piggybacking was normal and safe. Old Fairdale tenants didn't worry too much about holding the door open for someone coming in behind them. If it wasn't because of Christina, I wouldn't have been as jumpy. But I was.

Cautiously, I approached the door and glanced back at Tyler, who was engrossed in his video game.

There wasn't a peephole, so I opened the door slowly, holding it ajar, using half my body to hold it back in case anyone tried to shove it open. To my surprise, two people stood there, but to my delight neither of them was Christina. The man wore a police uniform, and the woman was dressed casually. What now? I thought. But I relaxed and held the door open a bit wider.

"Mr. Hall?" the woman asked.

"Yes. What's going on?"

"I'm Detective Nora Galovich from the Greenwood County Sheriff's Department, and this is Deputy Sheriff Lee Rivera. You are Ethan Hall, right?"

"Yeah," I replied nervously, stepping fully into view but using the door and my back to block Tyler from seeing them there. "What's this about?" I suspected I knew what this was about.

"Can we come in?" she asked, her tone serious.

I looked back nervously. "Well... my son..."

"Who's there, Dad?" Tyler called from inside.

"It will only take a moment, Mr. Hall," Galovich said. She then looked right behind me. I looked over my shoulder to find Tyler standing there wide-eyed.

"Hey, buddy," she said.

"Cool. Are you the police?" he asked.

Galovich smiled. "Sure am. Just need to talk to your daddy for a bit," she said, all friendly. She then addressed me more grimly. "We won't take too much of your time. I promise."

"Okay," I replied, trying to steady my voice as I stepped aside to let them come in. My mind raced. What had Christina done to get the cops to show up at my apartment unannounced on a Saturday morning?

I turned to my kid. "Go to your room, Tyler."

He glanced up at me, eyes still wide with curiosity, as he saw the police officers entering. "Dad? What's going on?"

"It's okay, buddy," I reassured him. "These officers just need to ask me some questions, so I'm going to try to help them out."

He looked uncertain but didn't argue, grabbing his handheld game console and disappearing quietly into his room.

Detective Galovich and Deputy Rivera settled on the sofa, and I sat across from them, my heart pounding in anticipation.

"So? What's this about?"

"Do you know Christina Garza?"

I knew it. What had she told them I'd done? Thoughts of the falsely accused Duke lacrosse players entered my head.

"Um, yes. We dated for about a month," I said.

"So you're no longer dating?"

"No. We stopped seeing each other a few days ago. What's this about?"

"Christina Garza's mother filed a missing person's report," Galovich began, watching my reaction closely. "Dana Garza says Christina went missing a few days ago, and she mentioned you were dating and that you were one of the last people to see her."

My mouth went dry, shock flooding through me. "Missing? Christina's missing?" My mind reeled. This wasn't possible. Christina was anything but missing; she'd been harassing me relentlessly.

"Yes," Galovich confirmed. "Her mother is very concerned. When was the last time you saw her?"

I'd never been questioned by the police before. It was nerve-wracking. Especially now that I figured they were eyeing me as a possible suspect. *Stop*, I told myself. *Suspect of what? I've done nothing wrong. If anything, I'm a victim of Christina, not the other way around.*

I composed myself internally and answered the question as calmly as possible. "Four days ago."

Galovich shot a side glance as the uniformed deputy who was jotting down notes. "Four days ago was the last time Christina's mother saw her. Or anyone else has seen her."

I felt flushed. And I didn't like the way she was looking at me. Like I was a criminal.

"What about at work? She was pretty high up over there," I asked.

"Same. She was a no-show one day, then quit over email the next day without notice."

"What? That doesn't make sense. She seemed very career oriented and responsible to me," I said.

The detective nodded. "Seemed that way. Until four days ago. You say you broke up on that day?"

I shifted in my chair, feeling like I was on a hot seat.

"We weren't exclusive, so not really a break up as in boyfriend and girlfriend. We were dating casually. Hooking up. She wanted to move our relationship to the next level, and I wasn't ready, so she got upset and ended things between us."

"How upset?" Galovich asked.

"Very," I said. "She wanted to move in together. We've only been dating casually for a month, so we were nowhere near for that stage in the relationship. I said no, and she got really pissed off. And I haven't seen her since then."

Galovich narrowed her eyes slightly, clearly skeptical. "You haven't heard from her at all?"

I hesitated—but I didn't like the way Galovich looked at me and talked to me. Despite everything Christina had put me, and Jade, through, I felt like I had no choice but to tell all to the cops, so I pulled the phone from my pocket. "Heard from her? Yeah, you could say that."

Anxiety gripped me as I handed my phone to Galovich and she read through the torrent of messages Christina had sent over the past few days. As the detective scrolled through them, her expression shifted from suspicion towards me to concern.

"Have you reported any of this to the police?" she asked, returning my phone.

I shook my head. "No. Honestly, I was hoping it would stop. I didn't want to get her into trouble with the police. Clearly, she's dealing with something."

Galovich exchanged another quick glance with Rivera, who hadn't said a word. She turned to me, and she was no longer giving me the hard look. Her expression softened briefly, but then she looked annoyed.

"This could have been addressed sooner and would have saved me leg work looking for her if you'd reported it. Harassment like this is serious. I suggest coming to the station and filing an official report," Galovich said curtly.

"Okay. I'll think about it," I replied quietly. I looked away but could feel her eyes rolling at me. But maybe now that her mother had gotten the police involved and reported her as missing, Christina would come back to her senses and finally leave me alone. What good would a police report do if that happened? I didn't want her to be arrested or go to jail if she stopped harassing me and Jade. I was willing to let bygones be bygones, so I wouldn't be rushing to the station to file that report. I wanted to play it by ear to see if she stopped messaging me.

Galovich and Rivera stood up, signaling the conversation was over. "Contact us immediately if anything escalates," Galovich advised. "And please consider coming to the station to file a report. These things don't typically go away without law enforcement involvement."

"I will," I agreed weakly, escorting them to the door.

I didn't tell them that Christina was also harassing Jade, nor that we suspected she had keyed Jade's car, even though we couldn't prove it. It was bad enough I had inadvertently placed Jade in Christina's crosshairs. I didn't want her to now also have to deal with the police.

Christina had to be lying low somewhere around town or in the more rural mountain towns, but she couldn't be too far since she had keyed Jade's car last night. She was around. How could the cops not find her? I couldn't shake the feeling that she was out there close by, watching me. Sending those messages. She had to be out there. Where the hell would she go if she wasn't in town? She wasn't close to her ex in San Francisco. And what about Robbie? Had she taken him with her or left him with Dana?

Tyler popped his head out from his room, interrupting my thoughts. "Are you in trouble with the police, Dad?"

"No." I put on a brave face and showed him my wrists. "See, no handcuffs. It's nothing. Just a misunderstanding between friends."

His eyes narrowed suspiciously, and I knew immediately I had another problem. Tyler would tell Kayla. The boy couldn't keep a secret. He told his mother everything, which was great, except at that moment, when I wanted him to keep my secret.

"Hey, Tyler," I said softly, kneeling in front of him. "It's important that you know everything's okay. But your mom might worry if you tell her the police came by without context, so let me talk to her first, all right?"

He shrugged, looking unconvinced. "Sure, Dad."

I sighed heavily as he returned to his room. The realization set in: I needed to tell Kayla everything before Tyler inadvertently did. And as uncomfortable as that conversation would be, it was nothing compared to my growing dread over what Christina might do next.

Reluctantly, I picked up my phone and called Kayla, pacing anxiously as it rang.

"Ethan," Kayla answered, sounding immediately concerned. "Tyler just texted me about the police showing up at your apartment just now. What's going on?"

That kid. Couldn't even wait a minute.

"I know," I said, running my hand through my hair nervously. "That's why I'm calling you. Look, Christina has been harassing me ever since I broke things off with her. I didn't want to worry you, but now the police are involved. Apparently, Christina is officially missing, but she's still sending me threatening messages."

"She's been threatening you and now she's missing, and you still had Tyler over for the weekend? Don't you think you should have told me?" Kayla said sharply, clearly upset.

And I was going to tell her she was overreacting, but I realized she wasn't. She was right to be upset with me over how I had been handling this situation.

"You're right," I admitted, my shoulders sagging with guilt. "I'm sorry, Kayla. I honestly thought I could handle it myself and it would blow over quickly. But I promise, Tyler was never in danger."

Kayla sighed deeply. "I think it's best to cut Tyler's visit short. Can you bring him home now?"

Disappointment filled me, but I knew she was right. "Yeah. I'll get his things and bring him over right now."

As I ended the call, my stomach twisted in knots. Everything was spiraling out of control, and I had no idea how to stop it. And where the hell was Christina hiding?

SIXTEEN
DETECTIVE NORA GALOVICH

Dana Garza lived in the mid-century modern ranch-style home on the outskirts of Whitlock. It was a quiet neighborhood where families kept neatly manicured lawns and maintained respectable appearances. The boxy structure with flat planes and clean lines avoided convoluted details and embraced the minimalist aesthetic that had been popular after the Second World War.

Dana eagerly welcomed me inside. I felt bad because she wasn't going to like the news I was about to deliver about her daughter Christina.

There is no easy way of telling a worried mother that her daughter isn't missing in the sense that requires police involvement. Christina's case had been classified as a voluntary missing persons case—and the proof was that she had been harassing Ethan Hall every day since she'd gone missing. And Christina was lucky Ethan had not pressed charges over the harassment, or the police would have to look for her not as a missing person but as a suspect in aggravated harassment.

Deputy Rivera accompanied me as we approached the front door. Dana Garza answered almost immediately, her face pale with worry, eyes searching ours for any glimmer of news.

"Mrs. Garza," I began gently, "can we come in? We need to discuss some updates regarding your daughter."

"Of course," Dana responded hurriedly, ushering us inside. She led us into a tidy, comfortably decorated living room with floor-to-ceiling windows that made me feel exposed. From the corner of my eye, I could see a fireplace mantel with a framed photograph of Christina and her son, Robbie, prominently displayed. My chest tightened slightly, knowing what I had to convey wouldn't be easy for any parent to hear. As a mother of two teenagers, I couldn't imagine not knowing where my children were, or whether they were safe. It didn't matter if the missing child was a teen like my kids or, like Christina, thirty years old. You never stop being a parent or worrying. But I had to push those thoughts away. Compartmentalization was an important component of a job where we often dealt with the worst parts of humanity.

She offered us something to drink, tea or water. Both the deputy and I politely turned her down. We sat down opposite Dana, whose nervous gaze shifted anxiously between Rivera and me. She clasped her hands tightly in her lap, clearly bracing herself.

"Please tell me you found her," she pleaded softly, desperation evident in her voice.

I glanced over at Rivera. We had agreed beforehand that I would do all the talking. So I took a deep breath, carefully choosing my words. "Mrs. Garza, we haven't found Christina, but we have confirmed she's been in regular contact with Ethan Hall and possibly others. Based on the messages Ethan provided, it appears your daughter isn't missing in the traditional sense. It seems she's voluntarily missing."

Dana stared at me in confusion, disbelief clouding her eyes. "What does that mean? That she took off on her own somewhere and hasn't reached out once this whole time, on purpose?"

I nodded and tried to provide more information, but Dana continued, now upset at the suggestion that Christina had done this on purpose.

"That's impossible. Sure, Christina and I have had our difficulties over the years, but she would never just abandon Robbie like this. He's only thirteen. She adores him."

Leaning forward, I spoke gently but firmly. "I understand why you'd feel that way, but abandoning a child isn't as uncommon as people think, especially if someone is experiencing significant personal distress and a mental health crisis."

"Distress?" Dana's eyes filled with tears. "What kind of distress could make her leave Robbie?"

"According to Ethan Hall, Christina had a difficult time accepting their breakup," I explained carefully, watching Dana. "He also shared with us that Christina was on medication for a bipolar disorder. You told us that she had a habit of getting off her meds, which had led to other incidents. She was arrested for disorderly conduct and placed on a 5150 hold."

"That was years ago." Her eyes narrowed as she looked at me with anger for mentioning it. But I had to dredge up these bad memories so she could accept what was going on.

"And this isn't the first time you've filed a missing report about Christina," I said gently.

"She was sixteen! She ran away from home. I didn't realize that would be held against her for the rest of her life," she snapped.

"It's not. It's just...Well, she has a history of taking off. She ran away to San Francisco when she was sixteen. And a couple times she went missing for a couple days," I said.

"She came home from San Francisco after a few days. And the other times, she went to healing retreats in Big Sur and Maui, but she would always check in after a day or two. She's never gone this long without letting me know she's okay or walking through that door apologizing. And that all happened before Robbie was born. She has always been there for her son. She got her life in order. An accounting degree. An MBA. A good-paying job. She would never walk away from all that."

I offered a thin smile. But I had to go on. "We learned she left her medication behind, and there are no recent pharmacy records showing she refilled her prescription. Is that correct?"

Dana nodded slowly, her shoulders slumping. "Yes, she's bipolar. Diagnosed years ago. She'd been managing it pretty well, I thought. But if she's off her meds..."

"Exactly," I continued gently. "Going off medication abruptly can lead to erratic behavior, poor decision-making, and emotional extremes. Ethan provided evidence of constant harassment via text messages from Christina, showing she's experiencing severe emotional distress."

Dana's face fell further, anguish mixing with confusion. "Harassment? Christina wouldn't do something like that. Are you certain?"

"Unfortunately, yes. We reviewed dozens of messages Christina has been sending to Ethan. They're intense, volatile, and extremely troubling. Ethan showed us messages sent as recently as two days ago, which confirms Christina isn't physically missing or in immediate danger."

"Her credit card and ATM card were used in Sebastopol, Eureka, and San Francisco," Deputy Rivera interjected gently.

"She appears to have taken off on her own accord," I added. "So right now, with the information I have, there just isn't much I can do. It's not illegal for an adult to go missing voluntarily."

Her breathing shaky as she tried to absorb the news, Dana said, "This doesn't sound like her at all. I can't imagine her doing something so malicious. Abandoning Robbie."

"People going through emotional crises can behave in ways that seem completely out of character," I said. "She might not be thinking clearly at the moment."

"You checked everywhere? How can she just vanish?"

"We've checked thoroughly," I assured her. "No sign of foul play or forced entry at her home. She withdrew cash before she disappeared, and there's been activity on her phone, obviously. And the recent card use. Given all that, we believe she's intentionally lying low."

Dana buried her face in her hands, shoulders shaking silently. My chest tightened with empathy. No mother should have to hear this.

"Look," I said softly, reaching out to touch her arm. "If Christina does come back or contacts you, please call us immediately. The best thing for her is to receive professional help. And for Ethan's and Christina's sake, we need to ensure her behavior doesn't escalate further than text messages."

Looking weary and defeated, Dana wiped her

tears. "Ethan should've reported this harassment sooner. Maybe we could have helped Christina earlier."

"He was reluctant to involve the police," I admitted. "He didn't want to get her in trouble. But now we know. Hopefully, she'll calm down and realize she needs help."

"I hope you're right," Dana whispered.

Deputy Rivera and I stood, preparing to leave. "Thank you for your time, Mrs. Garza," I said sincerely. "We'll stay in touch and we'll keep trying to make contact with Christina to make sure she's safe."

She nodded numbly, following us to the door. "Please find my daughter," she pleaded softly, tears spilling down her cheeks.

As we stepped outside into the bright sunlight, Rivera sighed deeply, shaking his head. "Tough one," he murmured quietly, echoing my own thoughts.

"It is," I agreed grimly. "But at least we know she's not physically missing. Just running."

"Think she'll come back on her own?" Rivera asked as we approached the patrol car.

"Maybe," I replied, my mind uneasy. "But something tells me this isn't over yet. People don't send those kinds of messages lightly."

Rivera nodded solemnly. "And if she doesn't?"

I paused, glancing back at the Garza house. "Then we have a real problem on our hands. Let's hope it doesn't come to that. She needs mental health treatment, not jail."

But as we drove away, a heavy feeling settled over me. Cases like these rarely got resolved in easy ways. Wherever Christina Garza was hiding, she was unstable, angry, and potentially dangerous. It wasn't a comforting combination.

I just hoped that Christina got back into therapy and back on her prescription before someone got hurt.

SEVENTEEN
ETHAN

The two following weeks were oddly calm, almost peaceful compared to the constant storm of harassment that had dominated my life before.

At first, I thought I was right. Christina stopped her shenanigans once the cops got involved. But a couple of days later, she started up again. But her barrage of text messages and emails had slowed way down. Each message was still venomous, but manageable. It was as if Christina had finally tired herself out. So I didn't go to the sheriff's department to file a complaint against her.

I had given up blocking her because she just came up with a new number and email address. The amount of effort she put into harassing me was mind-boggling. But for now, I was enjoying the relative respite.

A surprise outcome from all this was that I rekindled things with Jade. We kissed the day I went over to her place after her car was damaged. When the police came to my apartment, I stopped by her place after dropping Tyler off at Kayla's. And I felt down and out about having to tell my son that I was cutting his stay with me short, and that he wouldn't be spending much time at my apartment for now. The look on his face made it seem like I'd told him I didn't want to spend time with him anymore, though I said a million times that wasn't the case.

That night, Jade and I slept together again. She once again was wild and uninhibited. It was as if we were getting out our aggression and anger over what Christina had done to us with sex. We spent the entire Sunday at her place making love and watching movies. It was an intense reboot to our relationship, just like when we first met. Then we just started spending more and more time together again.

At first, it felt comforting. Jade and I bonded quickly over our shared ordeal with Christina, the conversations flowing easier than before now that we had something significant—and traumatic—in common. No one else knew what Christina had put me through but Jade, since she too was her victim. But as always, it was the wild sex that seemed to be the dominant force between us, and that thrill began to fade just like before.

I had to admit that we didn't have the connection needed in a romantic relationship. It couldn't just be physical. That spark that fuels couples wasn't there between us before, and it wasn't there this time around either. It was just missing, and there was no way to force that into existence. You either felt it or you didn't. And I didn't feel that way towards Jade.

So now that things had settled down and Christina had stopped harassing Jade, I felt it was time for us to once again go our separate ways, especially since I was no longer worried about Christina harming her physically.

As messed up as keying her car had been, I didn't think Christina would escalate to physical harm or in-person confrontation. Especially with her being on the cops' radar.

Christina seemed, after all, to have vanished from town, launching her attacks over text messages and emails. She had mentioned going to Hawaii every year to recharge; maybe she had gone there after keying Jade's car. Or, like I'd thought before, maybe it was just a bizarre coincidence and some juvenile delinquent had keyed the car. Jade didn't have security cameras, so there was no hard proof that it was Christina who had damaged her car.

Nevertheless, I felt things were calmer and safer, and that I could stop seeing Jade without having to feel guilty that Christina would attack her again.

Jade didn't seem worried about Christina anymore. Even when I told her about the cops showing up at my apartment to ask about Christina, she seemed put off by the police getting involved. She even asked me that day: "Did you mention me to the police?" Concern had crept into her voice.

"No," I assured her. "I didn't bring you up at all. They seemed satisfied once they saw the messages from Christina. I don't think they even believe she's truly missing anymore."

Jade relaxed visibly, sighing with relief. "Good. The last thing I need is to be dragged into some police investigation and be part of some odd love triangle." She blushed. "You know what I mean. They'll jump to some shitty conclusions about the three of us."

As we sat on Jade's couch watching TV, her head resting comfortably on my shoulder, I knew it was time to have the talk. I finally admitted to myself that this wasn't fair to her. I wasn't emotionally invested. I was using her as a shield, a comforting presence to ease my anxieties.

Two weeks had passed since the worst of Christina's harassment had faded, and now guilt tugged at my conscience. Jade deserved better than to be someone's emotional safety net.

"Jade," I said softly, shifting slightly so she sat upright, looking at me in confusion.

"Yeah?" Her eyes searched mine, as she sensed immediately that something was wrong.

I swallowed hard, finding it difficult to form words. "I think...I think maybe we should cool things off."

Her expression shifted instantly, confusion replaced by hurt. "What? Again? Why?"

"Look, we've been through a lot. Christina put us both through hell." I forced myself to meet her gaze. "But I don't think it's fair to either of us to continue this when I'm not fully invested. I'm still not interested in anything long term."

She pulled back slightly, eyes misting. "Are you serious, Ethan? We're good together. We've been doing so well."

"I know, but I just feel like I'm using you. It isn't right. You deserve someone who's fully present."

Jade shook her head slowly, disappointment etched clearly on her face. "I don't feel used. Ethan, I like what we have. I don't want it to end."

It was as I'd feared: She wanted more out of this relationship than I could give, like Christina; it wasn't right. I actually meant to be alone for a while. Just me and Tyler. I was going to temporarily hang up the dating app.

My resolve to be honest and decent didn't make things easier when I watched her looking at me, her face drawn, eyes glistening.

"Jade, please understand," I said, my heart twisting painfully. "With Christina still out there somewhere, still fixated on me, I just can't keep doing this. It's dangerous for you and not fair to either of us"

"You just want to go on with your hook ups. And I'm fine with that. Non-exclusive, right?" she said, trying hard to smile. It was obvious she was saying what I wanted to hear.

"I'm sorry. It's just not a good idea. I just want to spend time with my son and put this craziness with Christina behind me."

We sat in silence, the tension thick and heavy between us. Finally, Jade gave a quiet sigh of resignation. "Fine. If that's really what you want. I understand."

I reached out and gently hugged her, feeling her stiffen slightly before reluctantly relaxing into my embrace. "I'm so sorry, Jade."

She nodded against my shoulder. "Me too."

Feeling terrible for putting her through this again, I stood up and walked to the door. When I turned back one last time, she sat there, staring blankly at the TV, the light flickering across her disappointed face. I walked quietly into the night air with a strange mix of relief and guilt.

That night, as I lay in bed, sleep came fitfully. My dreams were restless, haunted by vague shadows and half-formed anxieties. I finally drifted off to sleep, but not for long.

The buzz of my phone jolted me awake on the nightstand. Groggy, I reached for it and squinted at the bright screen.

My heart immediately sank. Only Christina texted me in the dead of night.

I opened the photograph of a house engulfed in

brilliant orange and red flames, smoke billowing into the night sky. It took me a moment to figure out what this was about. Why would Christina send me an image of a house on fire? Then I bolted upright, adrenaline surging. I recognized the house—it was Jade's.

EIGHTEEN
ETHAN

I dialed Jade's number again. Straight to voicemail—again. Anxiety twisted painfully in my chest, making my heart pound like it wanted to escape my rib cage. Was this what a heart attack felt like? No, it had to be the beginning of a panic attack. I forced myself to take slow, deliberate breaths, but it helped little.

Snatching my wallet, keys, and phone from the nightstand, I jammed my feet into sneakers, not bothering to untangle the laces as they dragged over the floor. I bolted from the apartment, taking the stairs two at a time, each step echoing loudly in the empty stairwell, amplifying my panic.

Outside, the night air was cooler than I'd expected, biting through the thin cotton of my sweatpants and undershirt. It was what I had worn to bed, and in my haste to get to Jade's house, I hadn't thought about changing. I tugged at my windbreaker, frustration mounting when the zipper caught halfway up. After a sharp, angry pull, it finally gave way, and I hurried to my Jeep.

My hands trembled as I slipped into the driver's seat, clutching the FOB tightly and hitting the push-button ignition of my car. The engine roared to life, its familiar rumble offering no comfort. Tires squealed against the pavement as I sped up out of the lot and onto the empty street, my mind racing faster than the vehicle itself.

Horrific images flashed vividly through my head—Jade's house in flames, Christina's ominous message burned into my mind, the dark outline of a charred body hidden within. I rocked my head, desperately trying to banish those images, but they clung stubbornly, taunting me as I sped toward Jade's place.

I couldn't believe she would do this. Christina had escalated from harassment and vandalism to arson and... murder? I didn't want to even consider it, but why would anyone burn down someone's house in the middle of the night if they didn't want them dead? My stomach churned, nausea clawing at my throat. What if Jade had been inside? Fast asleep in bed. Home. It's where we all feel the safest. Our sanctuary from the outside world. I couldn't even imagine what Jade must have gone through when she realized her house was on fire. Had she woken up too late? I felt like throwing up as I pressed down on the accelerator.

If Jade was dead, it would be because of me. I was going almost seventy miles in a twenty-five-mile zone. I didn't care. I needed to get to Jade's house as fast as I could.

As I drove closer into Jade's neighborhood, the smoke became visible in the night sky, a sinister black plume billowing upward, glowing orange at its base. I couldn't believe my eyes.

I turned onto Jade's street, and my heart sank even further. Emergency lights flashed, red and blue streaks slicing through the darkness. Fire trucks, paramedic vehicles, and police cars crowded the road in front of me. I drove as close as I could until a patrol car blocked the way, its lights flashing an ominous warning.

Over to the side, I slammed the car into park. The vehicle jerked angrily at the abrupt stop. I barely remembered to shut off the engine and take the keys as I jumped out and sprinted toward the chaos. My legs felt numb, adrenaline pushing me forward despite the fear gripping my body.

The sidewalk was crowded with neighbors and onlookers, some wrapped in robes, blankets, others in their pajamas; their faces reflected shock, fear, and morbid curiosity. Nothing draws a crowd like a house fire. I ducked under the yellow police tape, desperate to reach Jade's burning house.

Seconds after I ducked under the tape, I heard someone yelling at me. It was a police officer who stepped directly into my path, holding his hand out to stop me. "Get back behind that tape, sir."

"That's my girlfriend's house!" I shouted frantically, my voice cracking with panic. "Please, I need to get to her. Is she okay?"

He glanced quickly at another officer, then back at me. "What's your girlfriend's name?"

"Jade Sommer. Please—is she all right?" I pleaded, nearly shouting over the noise of sirens and the crackling fire.

The officer exchanged a nod with his partner and reluctantly stepped aside and waved me through as he spoke into his shoulder radio.

I stumbled forward, closer to the scene of chaos. Flames roared, devouring Jade's house mercilessly as firefighters battled against the inferno. My face felt like I had stuck it into a hot oven. Another officer stepped directly in front of me, appearing concerned I was going to run into the burning house. "Are you the boyfriend?" he asked.

"Yes! That's my girlfriend's house! Jade Sommer. Is she okay? Please tell me she's okay!" My voice trembled. Fear overwhelmed every rational thought.

I heard a soft female voice behind me. "Ethan?"

The familiar voice snapped me out of my hysteria. I turned around, and my heart nearly stopped as relief washed over me. It was Jade; she was wrapped securely in a silver aluminum blanket, I assumed from the fire department. Her hair was a tangled mess, wet, and I could see ashes speckled throughout. Her eyes were red and watery. Her face was pale and smeared with soot, but she was alive.

"Oh my God, Jade!" I rushed forward, pulling her into a desperate embrace. She felt fragile, yet wonderfully solid in my arms.

She trembled slightly as she leaned into me, her voice quivering. "I don't know what happened, Ethan. The whole house... it just caught fire so fast. I barely got out."

I held her tighter. I could smell the smoke in her hair, dread returning in full force. I knew exactly what had happened and, worse, who had set fire to her house.

NINETEEN
JADE

THE FLASHING LIGHTS BLURRED TOGETHER AS I stood on the sidewalk, clutching the space blanket the firefighter had given me to keep me warm since I was in silk pajamas. It warmed me up, but I was shivering, not sure if that was from the cold or the shock as I watched firefighters battle the flames devouring my home.

My neighbors stood nearby, murmuring to each other, their eyes wide and faces illuminated by the ghastly orange glow. I could see them pointing in my direction. Even when I tried to ignore them, I could see them watching and pointing towards me as if to confirm to each other: *That's her house burning to the ground.*

I was kept away from them on the police side of the yellow tape, and I was grateful for that. I didn't want to be peppered with questions from neighbors I only knew from quick hellos and waves from our driveways.

I felt numb, shock setting in as I watched everything I owned crumble to ashes. Then I heard a commotion. The police interacting with someone. I heard a voice say my name and "girlfriend," and it very much sounded like Ethan. But that couldn't be. So I made my way over there and, sure enough, it was Ethan, and he was freaking out. I heard him shouting at the policemen that I was his girlfriend, trying to find out if I was dead or alive. Despite the horrors of that night and losing my house, barely making it out of it alive, I smiled. He had called me his girlfriend.

Girlfriend. The word replayed warmly in my mind. I hadn't felt certain about our status, even after the intimacy we'd shared recently. Yet, in the face of tragedy, Ethan had claimed me in public.

I overheard his panicked exchange with the officer, and a small thrill raced through me at the intensity in his voice. He cared. Ethan cared enough to rush over here, and the cops had to keep him from going inside to look for me.

I glanced toward the smoldering wreckage of my home. Was this what it took for Ethan to realize his feelings for me? Was I that desperate for his attention that I was smiling because I'd heard him call me his girlfriend? What was wrong with me?

I shook those intrusive thoughts away. I called his name, and he turned around. Relief washed over his face when he saw me standing there, and he came running to me.

His arms wrapped tightly around me, and I leaned into him, feeling a strange sense of triumph mingling with my grief.

"I'm here," he whispered softly into my hair. "You're not alone."

And despite the chaos, the loss, and the lingering dread, despite seeing my house engulfed in flames, in that moment I felt strangely at ease in his arms.

TWENTY
ETHAN

Jade's eyes, wide and glassy, reflected the chaotic red-and-blue lights flickering behind us. Thick, dark streaks beneath them reminded me bizarrely of a ball player's black eye grease. But I dismissed the thought instantly, focusing instead on the overwhelming gratitude at her being alive.

I held my arms around her but wasn't sure what to do or say.

"My house, Ethan. How could this have happened?"

My chest tightened. "Because of me," I said.

She looked at me, puzzled. "What do you mean? Wait. You think Christina did this? It had to be an accident. Faulty wiring or something."

"She texted me this," I said, showing the photograph of Jade's house on fire. "It's how I knew what was going on and how I got here right away."

Jade covered her mouth with her hands.

"I'm so sorry, Jade. This is all my fault," I said.

She looked at me, and I expected her to pull away from my embrace. To yell at me and tell me to get out of her life forever. I had dumped her twice, and now, because of Christina's obsession with me, Jade's car had been damaged and her house burned to the ground. But I was surprised that she cupped her hands around my face and looked at me with kind eyes.

"Don't say that. It's not your fault, Ethan. It's that crazy bitch. Not you. So don't beat yourself up over what happened here tonight. I don't blame you. I blame her." She then leaned up and kissed me gently on the lips. I didn't deserve such kindness from her. I would run for the hills if that was my house on fire and one of Jade's exes the prime suspect for arson.

A firefighter approached Jade, placing a hand on her shoulder.

"Miss Sommer, are you feeling any dizziness or shortness of breath?" he asked, his voice calm, professional.

Jade looked at the firefighter and then back at me. And she let out a stifled cough. And she nodded slightly, her eyes watering. "Yes, I feel dizzy and can't breathe very well."

"We should get you some oxygen, just as a precaution," he said. He waved over a paramedic crew, who placed an oxygen mask over her face and guided her toward an ambulance as they checked her vitals.

"Is she going to be okay?" I asked, anxiety once again tightening my chest.

The paramedic gave me a reassuring nod. "It's just precautionary. Smoke inhalation can be tricky, but she seems fine. You can follow us to the hospital."

As they loaded Jade into the ambulance, I pulled up the text—the image Christina had sent of Jade's house engulfed in flames. It was evidence. I quickly found the nearest officer, hands shaking as I showed him my phone.

"Detective Galovich needs to see this," the officer said gravely, forwarding the message immediately. The officer's phone rang right away. I heard his side of the conversation. "Yes, Detective. He's right here, but they took Ms. Sommers to the hospital, so he's heading over there. Okay. Will do, Detective." He hung up and looked up at me and told me that Detective Galovich would meet me at the hospital, so I drove there, adrenaline still surging through my veins.

The hospital waiting room was sterile and cold, bathed in harsh fluorescent lights that cast an unnatural glow over everything. A few other patients sat scattered around, their faces pale, exhausted, some clearly sick and waiting to be admitted. The muffled hum of medical equipment and low murmurs from the nursing station filled the space, an unsettling backdrop that amplified my anxiety.

At one in the morning, the ER was the last place where I wanted to spend any length of time, yet here I was, trapped in its sterile embrace. My head pounded relentlessly, a vicious combination of exhaustion and stress. I rubbed my temples, trying to ease the pain, but it persisted, a rhythmic throbbing in tune with the steady beep of a nearby monitor.

The warmth of the bitter hospital coffee seeped through the thin paper cup. It tasted awful, burnt and acidic, but at least the caffeine offered a lifeline, helping me cling to consciousness. Without it, I doubted I could stay upright much longer.

I glanced toward the ER doors, willing them to swing open with news about Jade, but they remained stubbornly shut, leaving me alone in my quiet agony. A few minutes later, someone called my name.

Detective Nora Galovich was standing by the entrance to the waiting room, a serious expression on her tired face. Seemed she, too, had been chased out of her warm bed that night.

"Let's talk back in here," she said, holding the door for me. I followed her silently to a small conference room tucked away in the hospital staff area.

Galovich closed the door behind us, and I felt suddenly claustrophobic. She motioned for me to sit. "Ethan, an officer sent me the message you received."

Her expression wasn't accusatory, exactly, but it revealed disappointment and frustration. I remembered her strongly urging me to file a police report against Christina, but I hadn't, and now this escalation.

"You failed to file a complaint against her like I recommended."

She stared at me intently, silently demanding an explanation.

"Detective, I—" I started, then paused, swallowing heavily. "I don't know what to say. Christina's been escalating, but I never thought she'd do something like this."

"Had you done it, we would have more than a missing person's report to go on, and we would have looked for her more thoroughly," Galovich asked, her voice steady but firm. "This situation could have been contained earlier, and maybe Ms. Sommer's house wouldn't have burned to the ground, with her almost in it."

Mixed emotions churned in me. Guilt over Jade's house but also anger towards the detective. As if filing a report about a bad break would send out the cavalry to find her and would have prevented this... I had my doubts. Jade hadn't made me feel responsible over what had happened, so why should the detective?

"I told you, I didn't want Christina to get into trouble," I said, staring into my empty coffee cup. "I genuinely thought she'd eventually stop on her own. And, honestly, I felt embarrassed. Like it was partly my fault for leading her on. But I had no idea she was capable of doing something like that. I don't think it's fair to blame me."

Across from me, Galovich sighed heavily. "I'm not blaming you. Look, I get it. Breakups can be messy. But when harassment turns violent, even if it's over the phone or on social media, if it's ignored, it usually gets worse. These matters rarely resolve on their own. That's why we have restraining orders and such at our disposal."

I nodded, shame burning hotly in my chest.

"How's Jade doing?" I asked, eager to shift the conversation away from myself.

"She's going to be fine," Galovich replied, her tone professional yet reassuring. "She wasn't seriously hurt—just shaken up. They'll be discharging her soon."

A thin, strained smile spread across my face. "Thank God."

Galovich eyed me carefully. "I spoke with her earlier. She mentioned Christina keyed her car a few days ago—and yet again, there wasn't a police report filed."

"Hold on," I said defensively, but my protest immediately faltered. That was exactly what had happened. Guilt stabbed at my gut, sharp and relentless. "We never thought it would escalate like this. I was so stupid. And now Jade's house is gone."

The detective studied me for a moment, her expression softening slightly. "Go easy on yourself, Ethan. Christina is the one responsible for this. But from here on out, we need your full cooperation. I want detailed records of everything she's sent you. Texts, emails, any interactions you've had online—no matter how small or harmless they seem."

I nodded, understanding the gravity of the situation. "I will send everything."

"You and Jade both need to come down to the station and file official reports. I'm also recommending you request a restraining order against Christina."

"Okay," I agreed quietly.

"Forward me everything—every text message, every direct message from Facebook, WhatsApp, Instagram—whatever platforms she's been using. Even messages that seem trivial. We need to build a strong case quickly."

I straightened up, determination slowly overtaking guilt. "I'll send you everything right away."

"Good." She rose from her seat, signaling the end of our conversation. "I know I've been hard on you. But try not to blame yourself. Stalking cases can be unpredictable. Christina clearly needs help. And now I have enough probable cause to go out and find her. And don't worry. I'll find her."

Back in the waiting area, I paced until Jade appeared, cleaned up and looking surprisingly composed, given everything she'd been through. She'd washed the soot from her face and brushed her hair. Seemed like she had even applied makeup, but I must be imagining that. Seeing her doing well lifted an enormous weight of guilt from my shoulders.

She smiled when she saw me, warmth flickering in her eyes. I pulled her into a tight embrace, breathing in deeply. She smelled faintly of hospital soap and smoke, but she was here and safe.

Galovich approached us again. "Where will you stay tonight, Jade? Do you have somewhere to go?"

Jade hesitated, uncertainty flickering across her features. Her gaze briefly met mine.

"She's staying with me," I blurted out, surprising myself. Jade's eyes widened slightly, a soft smile of relief forming on her lips.

Galovich gave us a firm nod. "Get some rest. Both of you. But get to the station to file those reports ASAP. I'll stay in touch with you two."

We reassured her we would and thanked her.

As we left the hospital, Jade looped her arm through mine and leaned close. The simple gesture filled me with a surge of protective warmth, though unease quickly shadowed it as my thoughts drifted back to Christina. What would she do next?

The air still held a sharp chill at 4:30 in the morning. On the horizon, the sky softened, brushed with the first faint streaks of dawn. It was a beautiful, peaceful moment—one most people missed while tucked in bed, oblivious. I yawned, feeling how heavily the night had settled over me. Sleep sounded incredibly appealing right now.

Jade squeezed my arm, interrupting my thoughts. "Are you sure about me staying with you, Ethan? I don't want to cause any more trouble."

I pressed her hand. "You haven't caused any trouble. You're staying with me. No arguments."

She smiled, a flicker of trust brightening her weary eyes. Still, anxiety gnawed at my gut. Christina had proven just how dangerous she could be. By inviting Jade to stay at my place, was I placing her in even greater danger? Putting myself at risk too?

But this was different, I reminded myself. Jade wasn't moving in permanently, not as my girlfriend or anything like that. This wasn't what Christina had wanted, the intimate arrangement I'd refused. No, this was different. I was helping a friend in need. It felt right.

Yet, deep down, I felt guilt. Despite everyone telling me otherwise, it was my fault Jade's life was now turned upside down. Christina had targeted her specifically to get to me, pulling Jade into chaos. And while I told myself it wasn't intentional, I couldn't ignore the harsh truth: I was responsible.

Jade tilted her head to look up at me, her eyes soft with hope and gratitude. My heart clenched. I needed to be careful. She had been through hell, and I wanted to support her, but not at the cost of sending mixed signals. I had to be clear about our arrangement: friends, nothing more.

TWENTY-ONE
ETHAN

Jade stood in the middle of my small apartment with an exhausted and vulnerable look on her face. During her previous visits, we'd have been clawing each other's clothes off by now—but tonight we stood in silence, the awkward silence stretching uncomfortably between us.

"Can I get you something to drink?" I asked, breaking the tension. "Diet Coke, orange juice, skim milk, or water?"

"I'm fine, thanks." She managed a weary smile, running a hand gently over her throat. "I must've had a gallon of water already; the smoke really dried me out. A shower sounds amazing, though. I cleaned up a bit at the hospital, but I'd love to wash off that antiseptic smell."

"Of course," I said, pointing down the hallway.

"You know where the bathroom and towels are." I hesitated, suddenly self-conscious. "Make yourself comfortable."

Jade caught my discomfort and smiled gently. "This is weird, isn't it?"

I laughed softly, relieved she felt the same way. "A little bit."

The shared laugh felt good, clearing some of the awkwardness lingering between us. I moved toward the bedroom, quickly returning with a pair of Tyler's sweatpants and one of my Lakers t-shirts. "Here, these might fit better than mine," I said, showing her Tyler's sweats. "And if you want, I can throw your clothes in the wash while you shower—get rid of the smoke and hospital smell."

Her eyes softened with gratitude. "That'd be perfect, thank you."

Then, without warning or embarrassment, Jade stripped off her clothing right there in the middle of the living room. My mouth went dry as she stood casually naked in front of me, holding out her clothes. I hesitated, trying to keep my eyes locked on hers and failing miserably. Heat crept up my neck.

She smiled, the corner of her mouth twitching slightly as she bit her lower lip, clearly aware of the effect she still had on me when it came to physical attraction. I quickly took her clothes and looked away, my face burning. Jade chuckled softly under her breath as she turned and walked toward the bathroom. The door closed gently behind her, leaving me standing there, dazed.

I exhaled slowly, shaking my head at myself as I crossed the room to the closet with the stacked washer and dryer. My mind raced. What exactly was she playing at? Or was I overthinking it? She'd stood there naked, eyes locked on mine. I wasn't overthinking it; she wanted to make love.

No, I couldn't go there. Not after all this shit going on. I was surprised that she would want sex after losing her house a few hours before.

While Jade showered, I busied myself in Tyler's room. I stripped the Minecraft Creeper Twin Comforter Set from his bed and replaced it with a neutral, plain white set. The domestic routine felt oddly grounding, even comforting, after the chaos of the evening.

My mind kept drifting back to Jade's unexpected little striptease, and I forced myself to push those thoughts away. She had just been through a traumatic experience, and I would not take advantage of her vulnerability. It was critical to draw clear boundaries. Whatever we'd had in the past—whatever intimacy we'd shared—must stay in the past. Tonight, she wasn't staying in my bed. She would sleep here, in the guest room.

The water shut off, jolting me from my thoughts. I

heard the bathroom door open a few minutes later, followed by Jade's footsteps softly padding outside the bedroom.

I stepped into the hallway, meeting her halfway. Her dark hair was damp, falling in soft waves over her shoulders. My t-shirt hung loosely from her frame, and Tyler's sweats were rolled at the waist. I realized how vulnerable and innocent she looked at that moment.

She caught my gaze and gave me a gentle, uncertain smile. "Thanks again for this, Ethan. It means a lot."

"Of course," I said, returning her smile warmly but carefully. "The guest room should be all set."

Jade hesitated briefly, as if considering saying more. Her face showed her disappointment at the fact that we weren't going to sleep together. Then she nodded and walked quietly into the room, closing the door behind her.

I stood there in the hallway, listening to the silence for a long moment. A mixture of relief and regret washed through me. I'd set the boundaries I needed, but part of me felt strangely unsettled, still haunted by the unspoken tension between us.

With a sigh, I turned and headed back toward my room, knowing sleep would be elusive tonight. But I was mistaken. As soon as my head hit the pillow, I was out.

Jade

I LAY in Tyler's bed, staring at the unfamiliar ceiling, frustration and humiliation squeezing my chest. Ethan's rejection cut deeper than I'd expected. It wasn't just sex I wanted—it was him. I wanted him to want me back, even if just for tonight. But now I felt like a fool.

I'd been naked for him, standing there exposed, vulnerable, offering myself openly—and he simply handed me clothes and disappeared to do laundry. It was mortifying. I'd tried to salvage my pride, thinking maybe he'd change his mind while I was in the shower. But no. When I'd stepped out, he'd just quietly guided me into his son's bedroom like I was a guest who'd overstayed her welcome. Even without sex, I didn't want to sleep alone tonight.

Replaying his gentle but firm refusal in my head, I tossed and turned, each memory bringing me fresh embarrassment. How desperate I must have looked! He probably thought I was pathetic, shamelessly throwing myself at him.

The worst part was that I hadn't even asked for commitment—just comfort, just closeness. But even that small mercy had been pulled off the table.

Unable to sleep, I sat up, pushing the hair away from my face. A picture frame sat on a small desk in the corner. Even in the dimness, I could make out Ethan's smile, Tyler's joyful expression, and Kayla's glowing face. The perfect family looking down at me—mocking me: the fool who kept throwing herself at a man who clearly still had feelings for his ex-wife.

Anger simmered under the humiliation. Why did Ethan have a photograph of his ex-wife proudly displayed here? Sure, this was Tyler's room and she was his mother, but Tyler was eleven—he wouldn't have put this framed picture up by himself. Ethan must've selected it, carefully placed it there, deliberately keeping Kayla's memory alive in this apartment.

Was that why he was so adamant about casual dating? Keeping me and even Christina at arm's length, refusing to commit because he still pined after Kayla? Or maybe it was Kayla herself—maybe she'd given Tyler this photo, manipulating things so Ethan would see her every single day, forcing him to remember their happy family.

My frustration boiled over. I climbed out of bed, moved across the room, and snatched the frame from the desk, turning it face down. The act gave me a small but hollow satisfaction. At least now I wouldn't have to look at their smug happiness.

Returning to the bed, I got under the covers, bitterness twisting inside me. I hated feeling like second-best, just a temporary distraction Ethan could discard at will. I deserved better than this. Ethan wasn't the only one who could choose—I could choose too.

Exhausted, emotionally raw, and unable to hold back the wave of sadness, I closed my eyes, wondering how I'd ended up here.

Sleep took a long time to come, and when it finally did, it provided no relief—only restless dreams of Christina looking scared and Kayla laughing at me.

TWENTY-TWO
ETHAN

The next morning I was groggy from the lack of a good night's sleep. A dull ache lingered behind my temples. It was already nine-thirty—late for me—but given the chaos of the previous night, I gave myself permission to sleep in. Thankfully, it was Sunday, which spared me from dealing with work while I processed the mess I was in, especially concerning Jade. Despite the sympathy I felt for her, the thought of her spending another night here felt increasingly uncomfortable.

I lay motionless, staring at the ceiling, unable to shake the vivid images from last night: Jade's house engulfed in flames, emergency lights flashing, her frightened eyes as she stood naked before me, her obvious disappointment when I showed her to Tyler's room instead of inviting her to mine. It was all too overwhelming.

With a sigh, I swung my legs off the bed, muscles aching in protest. Shuffling to Tyler's bedroom, I gently knocked on the partially open door.

"Jade?" I said hesitantly as I peered inside.

The room was empty. Jade had neatly made the bed. Had she been upset enough to leave saying nothing?

"Jade?" I called more loudly, moving quickly down the hallway toward the kitchen. The silence that met me confirmed what I already suspected: She was gone. Next to the coffee machine lay a folded note.

My stomach tightened as I unfolded the paper, recognizing Jade's handwriting.

Ethan, I care about you more than I should, and every time we're together, you hurt me without even realizing it. It's clear you don't care for me, and I can't just be friends with you, so I won't be bothering you anymore. Please don't reach out again unless you're ready to commit fully. Goodbye, Jade.

I read the note twice more, feeling both guilt and relief. The relief was shameful, but I couldn't deny its presence. Jade had left, taking control of a situation I had struggled to navigate. Had I done right by pushing her away, or was I just selfishly avoiding responsibility? What if Christina targeted her again?

Before I could untangle my thoughts further, my phone rang. Kayla's name flashed urgently across the screen.

"Hello?" I answered cautiously.

"Ethan, what the hell is going on?" Kayla's voice trembled with controlled anger. "I just saw the news. Jade's house burned down? And you were there? Care to explain?"

I hesitated, trying to catch up. "How did you—"

"There's a video on the news website, Ethan! You're standing there with your arm around Jade. They're saying the fire might be suspicious. So what the hell happened?"

"Kayla, calm down," I pleaded softly, though I could not hide my nervousness. "Yes, Jade's house burned down. The police think Christina's behind it. Jade barely got out alive."

"Oh my God, Ethan," she whispered, genuine fear replacing anger. "Why didn't you call me right away? Tyler was just with you! Do you have any idea how dangerous this is?"

"I planned to tell you today," I mumbled, realizing how insufficient that sounded. "Jade just left. She left a note—she needs space. It's probably best this way."

"Right now, I don't care about Jade," Kayla snapped. "I care about our son. Tyler can't be around you until Christina is found. I won't risk his safety."

"Kayla, please—"

"No, Ethan," she cut me off, decisive and unyielding. "This is non-negotiable. Call me when this mess is sorted."

She hung up, leaving me holding my phone tightly, helpless and angry. I wanted to call her back, to argue, but the thought of Tyler being endangered because of my drama silenced me.

My apartment felt suffocating, the walls pressing inward. I needed air.

Deciding breakfast might help, I drove to the local diner. The familiar smell of greasy food provided little comfort as I pulled up the news site Kayla had mentioned. Sure enough, there was the video: Jade shivering in a reflective blanket, my arm protectively around her, emergency lights illuminating our haunted faces.

The reporter's voice echoed in my ears, labeling the fire as "suspicious," highlighting the small-town drama for all to see. Fairdale didn't have its own TV station, but Eureka's local news served as the region's gossip mill, broadcasting across the Redwood Empire. My heart sank as I realized how many people—including my coworkers—might see this.

Anxiety churned in my stomach, spoiling the omelet I had ordered. My boss would certainly have questions on Monday. The thought made me queasy, forcing me to push away the half-eaten breakfast. I leaned back, closing my eyes and exhaling deeply, wishing this nightmare would end.

As I sat there finishing my coffee, I couldn't help but wonder where Jade had gone. Maybe she'd checked into a hotel somewhere in town—or perhaps she'd decided to stay in one of her house-flip properties. She had mentioned before that she usually had at least one or two projects going. It wouldn't be unusual for her to use one of those places in a pinch, especially since her house was now completely uninhabitable. Given the extent of the damage, it would likely take months—maybe even a year—to demolish and rebuild on that lot.

One thing I was certain of was that she wouldn't be staying with family. She'd mentioned once that she grew up near Modesto but was always cagey about sharing details. Whenever I'd asked her about her family—basic getting-to-know-you questions when we'd first started seeing each other—she quickly changed the subject. Her parents were deceased, she told me flatly, and she was an only child. The topic was obviously a sensitive one, so I let it go. She also had children in Maine, but in the short time we'd been involved, she never once visited them. A sadness lurked there, something hidden just beneath the surface that made me think Jade's past held secrets she wasn't eager to revisit.

After paying the check, I walked back to my car and reached into my jacket for my keys. My fingers brushed against something else in my pocket. Curious, I pulled it out. Detective Galovich's business card. As I stared at the card, the urgency of my situation crashed over me again. I'd been putting it off, not wanting to escalate things further with Christina. But now there was no other option. The chaos of last night had convinced me beyond a doubt: This situation would only end when Christina was behind bars.

I dialed Galovich's number. My life was spinning dangerously out of control, and I couldn't pretend things were normal anymore.

It was time to do what I should have done weeks ago: file an official police report.

TWENTY-THREE
ETHAN

By five in the morning, I was awake, so I just got out of bed. I felt a dread that I couldn't shake. I thought about calling in sick at work. I didn't want to be gossip fodder for coworkers who had seen the news report video and watched me at the fire talking with the police or read the article in *The North Coast Examiner*. I didn't want to tell them about my private life.

But being busy at work was the distraction from all the chaos that I actually wanted, so as not to think about all this. I emailed my supervisor to let him know I would be an hour late because I would stop at the sheriff's department on my way to work to file the report against Christina once and for all.

I was brewing a pot of coffee when my phone buzzed. A blocked number, so I knew it was her. I looked at the message, which was an image file.

Christina had taken a screenshot of the news video from the fire that captured me and Jade, my arm around her as I tried to comfort her. She had cropped it and zoomed in on Jade and me, drawn ridiculous devil horns atop my head, and scrawled the word ASSHOLE boldly in angry-red digital ink. The word WHORE stood prominently above Jade's head with an eggplant emoji provocatively placed near her mouth. Childish, yes—but in context, deeply unsettling.

Despite my better judgment, fury and helplessness pushed me to respond: *You almost killed her. You are sick in the head. Harass me all you want, but leave Jade alone. You've done enough.*

Her reply chilled me to my bone. *You let that skanky whore move in with you, but not me. Go to hell.*

She knew Jade had spent the night. Christina was watching me—us. The reality of her proximity, of her eyes lingering nearby, was terrifying. Fairdale was tiny, home to barely a thousand residents. How could Christina evade the police in such a small place?

My anger took control again. I fired off another text before I could stop myself. *Because you burned her house to the ground, psycho.*

Christina's response was immediate: *You have seen nothing yet.*

My heart pounded as I waited impatiently in the lobby of the Greenwood County Sheriff's Department. I was greeted by Deputy Rivera, who had me file a police report on the harassment and stalking Christina had subjected me to. It felt cathartic to list everything she had been doing, reminding me of how out of hand this had all gotten and how quickly she had turned from a sweet, kind girl to a vile monster right out of *Fatal Attraction*.

I handed the report over to the deputy, who thanked me as he went towards the back of the station. I sat alone for about ten minutes, marveling that the only thing worse than hospital coffee was the police station one.

Detective Galovich finally appeared, motioning me into her cramped, cluttered office.

"Thanks for seeing me," I said, my voice tight with tension.

"Of course," Galovich replied, taking her seat across from me, looking professional but concerned. "I looked over your report. So Christina texted you last night."

Without hesitation, I showed her Christina's latest disturbing text, the edited photograph flashing grotesquely on my phone screen. Galovich leaned forward, squinting at the image, her brows furrowing as she studied it carefully.

"This is disturbing," she muttered, troubled. "She keeps escalating."

Escalating? She set a damn house on fire with Jade in it. How could they not have found her yet? I nodded, my throat dry. "She knows Jade stayed at my apartment the night of the fire. She's stalking me. So she's obviously in town. Have you found her?"

Galovich sighed, leaning back, fingers steepled thoughtfully beneath her chin. "We've been actively searching for her, but there's been no sighting. No credit card transactions in weeks, nothing substantial. It's like she vanished, but obviously she's close."

"What about all these text messages? Can't you ping her location?"

"You're in IT, Mr. Hall. If someone is tech-savvy enough, they can cover their digital tracks pretty well, and Christina has been very good at it. We think she might not be in Fairdale or even in the state."

"She's here, Detective," I insisted, my frustration boiling over. I showed her the text message she had just sent me.

"We're doing everything we can," she assured me calmly, although the frustration showed faintly in her eyes. "I know you feel helpless, but engaging her by sending her a text wasn't very smart."

"I couldn't help it," I admitted quietly. "She burned Jade's house down. She nearly killed her. What's next?"

Galovich held my gaze steadily. "We're stepping up patrols, keeping a close eye on your apartment. How long will Jade be staying with you?"

I shifted in the hard chair uncomfortably. "She's actually not staying with me anymore. Just last night."

"So, where is she staying?" she asked with raised brows.

"I don't know. I woke up this morning, and she was gone."

Galovich looked at me like she didn't believe me.

"She slept in the other room. I was exhausted in my room with the door closed, so I didn't hear her leaving."

"I see. And you haven't seen or talked to her since she left?"

Galovich made me wonder if cops got trained to look at you in a way that made you feel like an insignificant ant, because she had that look down pat.

"We decided not to see each other romantically. It was my idea, and she wasn't happy about it. She left without waking me up, leaving a note asking me not to bother her, so I'm respecting her request."

"I understand. I'll reach out to her to find out where she's staying so I can have a patrol unit drive by her place at night as well. Just in case Christina tries something else."

"Great, thank you. Even though we're not seeing each other, I worry about her with Christina out there somewhere thinking I'm back together with Jade," I said.

The detective gave me a curt nod before she got up and shook my hand. "Thank you for stopping by and filing the police report. But please, Ethan, no more communicating with her. Every interaction gives her power."

"I understand."

I got back in my car and banged on the steering wheel out of frustration. Christina's chilling promise lingered in my head:

You haven't seen anything yet.

TWENTY-FOUR
ETHAN

I PULLED INTO THE PARKING LOT OF FITZEK Manufacturing and slipped into my usual spot. Normally, arriving at work was a mundane ritual, something I barely thought about—but today was different. My nerves were raw from the weekend, and dread settled over me like a heavy blanket.

As soon as I stepped through the glass doors into the lobby, I felt it—the sudden, unmistakable shift in atmosphere as people saw me enter. Conversations stopped abruptly, replaced by awkward silence. Eyes darted toward me, then quickly looked away, pretending interest in anything but my presence.

Near the reception desk, a group of coworkers whispered quietly, glancing in my direction before looking back down at their phones. One of them giggled, hastily smothering the sound with a cough. Unease spread through me like ice water.

Great, I thought bitterly. Gossip traveled faster than wildfire in a small town like Fairdale. At barely ten in the morning, my personal life had already become office entertainment. This was going to be one hell of a long day.

I quickened my pace toward the elevators, hoping to escape the lobby's oppressive awkwardness. But before I reached them, Mario, the building's security guard, stepped directly into my path. He was usually friendly, quick with a joke or a smile. Today, though, his demeanor had shifted. He stood rigidly, eyes flickering around the lobby, avoiding mine. A deep frown creased his normally relaxed face.

"Um, Mr. Hall?" he said hesitantly, keeping his voice low. He shifted, clearly dreading whatever he had to say next. "I—I have a message for you."

A wave of apprehension crashed over me. My mouth went dry. "Mario, what's going on?"

He finally looked at me, pity clear in his eyes. "They're waiting for you in conference room B."

I blinked to ward off panic. "Who's waiting for me?"

Mario hesitated, as though reluctant to say the words aloud. Finally, he said, "Management and HR."

My heart sank. Human resources and management didn't hold meetings together unless it was serious—or very bad news. I felt suddenly nauseous.

"HR wants to see me?" I asked again, needing to be certain.

He nodded gravely. "They're already waiting. Please, come this way."

I knew where conference room B was located. Every employee knew that room by reputation, even if they'd never been inside. Around the office, they called it "the chopping block"—the place reserved exclusively for the meetings that ended careers, hidden away from prying eyes and curious glances.

Unlike the bright, open conference rooms upstairs, with glass walls and spectacular views of the mountains, conference room B was windowless, tucked discreetly off the lobby, and close to the building's entrance. Management used it specifically for private, sensitive conversations—terminations, layoffs, disciplinary meetings—away from curious eyes, easy for employees to leave discreetly afterward.

My footsteps echoed in my ears as Mario led me across the marble floor toward the room. Each step felt heavier than the last, dread tightening its grip around my throat. I'd only been at Fitzek Manufacturing for a couple of months, so I was still a new employee, but I thought I was doing well at my job. I hadn't received reprimands or warnings. But my gut told me that whatever awaited me behind that door had nothing to do with performance metrics or my brief tardiness this morning.

Mario stopped outside the door, knocking quietly. Without waiting for a response, he turned and gave me one final, sympathetic look before quickly retreating to his station at the lobby desk, as if he couldn't bear to watch what happened next.

I took a deep breath, trying to steady my nerves, and opened the door.

Inside, the small, windowless room already felt claustrophobic. Three pairs of eyes looked up, their expressions grim and uncomfortable. Andrew, my direct supervisor, shifted in his chair uneasily, refusing to hold my gaze. Laura Bennett, Andrew's boss, regarded me coolly, her face an unreadable mask. Across the table, Hannah Gutierrez from HR sat with a manila folder already open in front of her.

"Please, have a seat, Ethan," Hannah said, her voice soft but authoritative. The door clicked shut behind me with finality.

I swallowed hard, lowering myself into the chair, feeling small and helpless. "What's going on?"

Laura folded her hands calmly on the table. She seemed almost practiced in delivering bad news, her voice steady and emotionless. "Ethan, this morning at approximately six a.m., an email was sent to every employee in this company. All 357."

An icy chill trickled down my spine. I already knew what was coming, even as my mind fought desperately to deny it.

Andrew shifted again, finally meeting my eyes with a look of profound embarrassment. "The email included a video. It was extremely explicit—showing you and a woman in a compromising position."

So this wasn't about the fire? I glanced down at the folder she had opened. There was a printout with a screenshot of me. It was cropped so only my face was visible, but I recognized where they had screenshotted it from instantly. It was the sex tape Jade and I had recorded when we first started hooking up. It had been her idea. It was supposed to be private between her and me. I couldn't believe it. That video was sent to work?

Oh God. The room spun around me. Shame burned hot across my face. I could hardly breathe. This wasn't possible. But deep down, I knew it was Christina. She had somehow hacked into Jade's devices or mine and stolen it. She'd finally done it: She'd found the perfect way to ruin me.

"That was private. I didn't send that," I stammered weakly. "I'm being stalked. Harassed—"

Hannah raised a hand gently, cutting me off. "We understand your personal situation may be complicated, Ethan. Unfortunately, our company policies are very clear on matters like this. The CEO himself reviewed the situation this morning."

I already knew what was coming next, but it still hit me with physical force.

Laura looked me in the eye. "We have no choice but to terminate your employment, effective immediately."

Frozen, numb with shock and humiliation, I sat barely comprehending their next words. My thoughts raced desperately, searching for some way to protest or appeal, but their expressions were resolute. The decision had been made.

In that moment, I realized Christina had taken everything from me—my dignity, my security, and now even my livelihood. I'd lost everything I'd worked so hard to build, and I was powerless to stop it.

"What about my things?" I asked weakly.

"Andrew packed your belongings. You can pick them up at the front desk on your way out," Hannah informed me softly.

I left the room in stunned silence, feeling the weight of my humiliation press down upon me with every step toward the exit. I didn't dare to look up, too humiliated to make eye contact with anyone. I've never been fired before. Had never had problems at work going back to my first job ever at fifteen at the In-N-Out Burger near LAX.

Everything I'd worked for, destroyed by a single malicious act. A most intimate moment recorded for just the two of us had now been viewed by hundreds of people. I swallowed hard, feeling like I was going to vomit.

My life had unraveled completely, and now Christina had stripped me of even my dignity and of my employment.

How was I going to explain this to Kayla? And although she worked for the hospital, my health benefits were much better, so I had Tyler under my insurance plan. I had not only lost my job, but Tyler's health benefits. I felt my legs wobbly as I made my way to the car. I couldn't look back at the building, convinced everyone was staring at me in disgust. I tossed the banker's box with my things into the back and jumped inside. Driving away, I was too embarrassed to even look at my former place of employment in the rear-view mirror.

I pulled into my parking spot at my apartment and sat in my car for a minute. I still felt sick to my stomach.

Why would Christina, who had professed to love me, do all this? Why would you hurt and destroy someone you supposedly loved?

Sitting behind the wheel, my phone buzzed. My heart sank further as an unknown number flashed on the screen. I knew it was her. She probably wanted to rub it in my face what she had just accomplished with the click of the email send button.

You look so sad, the message read, accompanied by a mocking wink emoji.

My head whipped around frantically, paranoia gripping me. Where was she hiding? Fear swiftly shifted to rage. I threw open the car door, stepping out onto the pavement, fury blinding me.

"I'm here, you crazy bitch!" I shouted, my voice echoing in the parking lot. But there was no response, only silence and the disapproving stares of distant neighbors. I slammed the door shut and grabbed my box from the trunk, slamming that as well, and went into my apartment.

Christina was intent on destroying my life and Jade's. The police seemed incapable of stopping her. Hell, they couldn't even find her. I would not sit around waiting for Christina's next dirty move.

I went into my bedroom and pulled out a suitcase from the back of my closet. I opened it. Wrapped in my spare bed sheets was a small locked safe. I entered the code and opened it. Inside was my Ruger .380 automatic pistol and a box of ammunition.

TWENTY-FIVE
ETHAN

I drove a few miles out of town to the only gun range near Fairdale. My Ruger .380 automatic lay securely in its case on the passenger seat. It had been years since I'd fired it. I'd bought it when a rash of home invasions swept across the state and there was nonstop news coverage emphasizing rising crime rates in Los Angeles. Kayla was furious when I brought it home, worried about Tyler's safety, but I insisted. It was for our protection, a last resort. I kept it locked in a gun safe and kept that hidden and out of the reach of Tyler. But even if he found the safe, he didn't have the code to open it.

I never imagined I'd feel the urgent need to practice shooting again, especially after moving to Fairdale. But Christina's actions left me little choice in the matter.

Inside the range, the smell of gunpowder and oil

hung thick in the air. I had cleaned the gun before heading over here. I enjoyed the soothing ritual of getting out the kit and cleaning the gun.

Then I loaded the magazine methodically, each cartridge sliding in smoothly, clicking into place.

At the firing line, I raised the pistol, aiming at the target downrange. My hands shook slightly; adrenaline surged. The first shot was loud, startling me even with ear protection on. The recoil jolted my wrists. I steadied myself, took a breath, and fired again. And again. Gradually, muscle memory returned. My confidence grew with each successive round hitting closer to center mass.

When I finally left the range, I felt calmer. Part of me hoped that if Christina was out there somewhere stalking me, she would do so on the way to the gun range. I was determined to protect myself and my family from Christina's madness, and I was willing to do whatever it took.

Back at my apartment, my phone buzzed, rattling across the kitchen counter. Jade's name flashed on the screen. My heart sank—I'd debated reaching out to her after what had happened this morning but respected her request for space. Did she know Christina had stolen our private tape and made it public? I had been dreading this call.

"Hello?" I said with caution.

"What the fuck, Ethan?" Jade's tone was sharp.

I sighed heavily. "You saw it?"

"Yes, Ethan! It was sent to several real estate and mortgage brokers I work with. And to my graphic design clients. My professional reputation is ruined. That video was supposed to be private. How the hell did that crazy bitch even get it?"

"I've been asking myself the same thing. Christina's obviously more tech-savvy than I realized. Burner phones, proxy servers... she must have hacked into our cloud storage or phones and downloaded it."

"Unbelievable." Jade groaned. "I can't believe this is happening."

"She emailed the video to everyone at work, so they fired me this morning."

"Oh, Ethan," Jade said, softening. "I'm sorry."

"I went to the police and filed a report. I also requested an emergency restraining order."

"You did?" Jade sounded genuinely surprised.

"Yeah. After everything she's done, the gloves are off. Detective Galovich called what she did with our video 'revenge porn.' And that's illegal in California, intentionally distributing private intimate images without consent. So Christina keeps getting in more and more deep trouble, assuming the police ever find her."

Jade was silent for a moment. I could hear her breathing heavily on the other end. "God, Ethan, I don't know what to do."

"You need to protect yourself," I warned. "Christina's dangerous and obviously deranged. Who knows what she'll do next?"

"How do you mean, protect myself?"

"I own a handgun," I admitted. "I just dug it out of my closet and went to practice shooting. Do you have one?"

"No," she replied, sounding stunned. "You own a gun?"

"Yes. It's for protection. Maybe you should get one. There's a ten-day waiting period, so don't think too long. I can show you how to use it at the range."

Jade paused. "I don't know, Ethan. Guns make me nervous."

"Christina makes me nervous," I countered. "Just think about it, please. So, yesterday I got your note. I'm sorry—"

She cut me off. "I don't want to talk about that right now."

"Okay, I understand. Where are you staying?"

"At my mountain property, ten miles from town, I was getting it ready as a short-term rental. So I'll put that on the back burner, and I'll stay there until I figure out what to do next. It's pretty secluded, so I'm actually enjoying the peace and quiet."

"That's good. Secluded might be safer right now."

She sighed again. "What are you doing tonight?"

I grimaced, dreading what lay ahead. "I'm going to Kayla's. I need to warn her before she receives a copy of that damned video."

"Oh," Jade replied in a whisper. I suspected she wanted to see me, perhaps hook up. But I said nothing. "Good luck with that," she finally said.

"Yeah," I muttered. "I'm going to need it."

My heart raced at the thought of facing Kayla. I told her we needed to talk. She pressed me for details. I told her it was about Christina, but that I wanted to tell her face to face. Besides, I missed Tyler, and I wanted to at least spend some time with him even if it was just a quick visit.

She was reluctant but agreed to have me over at seven p.m.

I put the gun safe back in the closet since I didn't have a concealed carry license, grabbed my coat and left the apartment. Now I couldn't help but look around like I was a soldier on patrol, wondering just where the hell Christina was hiding and wondering if I was stepping out to an ambush.

TWENTY-SIX
ETHAN

The drive to Kayla's place shouldn't have felt long—nothing up here ever really felt too far—but tonight, every mile dragged out endlessly. My mind was spinning with worry.

At first, Kayla's farmhouse had seemed idyllic, like something from a postcard—rolling fields, rustic charm, quiet serenity. But now, with Christina lurking somewhere, I hated the isolation. Her closest neighbors were half a mile away, and the police or sheriff were a good fifteen minutes out. The thought made my stomach clench with fear.

Images of Kayla and Tyler flashed through my mind—laughter echoing through the house, lazy weekend mornings, peaceful evenings by the fireplace, a sense of warmth and completeness that felt like a distant memory. How had everything fallen apart so completely?

Christina's viciousness toward Jade terrified me. If she could be so ruthless with someone she'd only met once, what would she be capable of doing to Kayla? My chest tightened at the thought. Even though they'd never met, would Christina hate Kayla because we were married? I didn't want to let my mind go there. I divorced Kayla, so why would Christina go after her? But the thought terrified me because I would not only have put Kayla in danger, but Tyler.

I finally pulled into Kayla's driveway; her car was parked outside. The soft glow of lights through the window sent a pang through my chest. An overwhelming desire to protect her, to make sure no harm would ever come to her or Tyler. The ache felt raw, urgent, powerful.

I stepped out into the cool evening, the fresh air momentarily steadying me. My pulse quickened as I knocked on the front door. I hoped my expression wouldn't betray how rattled I felt.

Kayla opened the door, her dark eyes worried yet warm, and for a second I was struck once again by how beautiful she was. Even now, after everything, just seeing her was comforting.

"What's going on now, Ethan?" she asked without preamble, brow furrowing slightly.

Before I could respond, Tyler came barreling down the stairs, his face brightening instantly when he saw me.

"Dad!" he exclaimed, wrapping his arms around

my waist in a tight hug. I hugged him back, holding on to him longer than usual, savoring the innocent, uncomplicated joy of the moment.

Kayla's tense expression softened as she stepped aside, allowing me to come inside the warm glow of their home. "Come on in. Do you want a soda?"

I smiled gratefully, my throat suddenly dry. "Yeah, thanks."

As Tyler released me, I studied him, ruffling his hair. "How was school today, bud?"

His grin faltered into a dramatic scowl. "I hate school."

Despite my anxiety, I chuckled. Kayla returned from the kitchen, handing me the cold soda, our fingers briefly brushing. It felt comforting, yet strangely bittersweet.

We spent about ten minutes chatting with Tyler about his classes, his teachers, and his complaints about homework. Then, reluctantly, I put a hand on his shoulder.

"Hey, Ty, can you give your mom and me a minute? We've got some boring adult stuff to talk about."

"No problem," Tyler said easily, shrugging. "My friends are waiting for me on Discord anyway."

"Discord?" I asked, half amused and half bewildered. Times had certainly changed since I was a kid.

"It's just a voice chat thing, Dad," he explained, shaking his head as if I'd just asked him what color the sky was. Then he bounded upstairs, disappearing quickly into his room.

Kayla glanced at me, a faint smile tugging at her lips. "He spends too much time online, doesn't he?"

I sighed, taking a sip from the soda. "Yeah, but at least he has friends he enjoys hanging out with—even if it's virtual."

A brief silence settled between us. I couldn't help but notice how different things were here. In my cramped apartment, there was never space to speak openly without Tyler overhearing. But here, in this sprawling old farmhouse, privacy was easy to find.

Kayla sat across from me in a chair, her posture rigid, arms folded defensively. When we were married, she would always sit beside me on this very couch. Now the distance between us felt symbolic.

"What's she done now?" Kayla's voice was calm but strained, her eyes wary.

This was painfully awkward—like confessing infidelity, though we'd been divorced for nearly a year. "She sent a video...a private video of..." I trailed off, swallowing hard, embarrassment hot on my face. "Me and Jade."

Kayla's eyes widened, comprehension dawning swiftly. "Oh my God, Ethan. Who did she send it to?"

"My job," I said quietly, shame tightening my throat. "She used the entire employee email list. Everyone got it, from the CEO down to the cleaning crew."

"No." Her voice dropped to a stunned whisper. "She wouldn't."

Unable to look away from her horrified expression, I nodded slowly. Tears pricked behind my eyes, threatening to spill. "She did. They fired me this morning."

"What?" Kayla sat forward, outrage replacing shock. "How could they do that? You're the victim here."

"I said exactly that, but they didn't care." My voice trembled. "Kayla, I'm sorry—Tyler's health insurance—"

"Don't worry about that," she interrupted. "I can put him on my work plan. It's fine. But this woman—she's completely unhinged."

"I went to the police. Detective Galovich said Christina's racking up serious charges. If they ever manage to catch her, she'll be locked up for a long time."

"Can she really evade the police forever?" Kayla asked, leaning back.

"I don't know. Honestly, I'm not sure the Greenwood County Sheriff's Department can handle someone like her."

"You'd be surprised," Kayla said. "Don't let sleepy little Fairdale fool you. There are plenty of criminals hiding in these mountains. All those marijuana farms, illegal growers, fugitives—they keep the sheriff's department busier than you'd think."

"This isn't exactly the usual crime around here," I said. "She's smart. She's tech-savvy, careful."

Kayla studied me, eyes narrowing. "Do you think she's still nearby?"

I hesitated. Christina had made it clear in her messages that she wasn't far. "It's a big county with lots of remote places to lay low."

For a long moment, Kayla's face remained tense, pensive. Then suddenly her lips twitched, and a suppressed giggle escaped.

"You're laughing?" I asked, incredulous.

She burst into a full laugh, shaking her head. "Sorry, Ethan—but you? A sex tape? You were always such a prude. I never imagined."

Heat rushed to my cheeks. But the laughter was contagious, and soon I chuckled alongside her. For a moment, just a brief moment, the tension lifted, and I could breathe again. It had been too long since I'd laughed.

Yet even as I laughed, I knew this reprieve wouldn't last. Not while Christina was still out there.

TWENTY-SEVEN
DETECTIVE NORA GALOVICH

THE FRUSTRATION I FELT OVER THIS CASE WAS relentless, an itch I couldn't reach to scratch. Sitting at my cluttered desk in the Greenwood County Sheriff's Department, I stared at folders and notes scattered haphazardly across the surface—evidence of my relentless but fruitless pursuit of Christina Garza. Every lead, every tip had dissolved into dead ends, and the case felt more elusive by the day.

Christina Garza had become a ghost, a puzzle with pieces that refused to fit together. Her mother, Dana, called me almost every day asking if I had found her daughter. I suppose even if she were arrested and in jail, that would bring a sense of relief to her mother and son. They'd know, at least, that Christina was alive. Although finding her was my top priority right now — the only active case I was working on — I was starting to wonder if I was looking for a master criminal or a body.

I rubbed my weary eyes, fighting off the exhaustion that had haunted me for days. How could a mild-mannered accountant with a spotless record—no traffic violations, no misdemeanors, nothing—transform overnight into a cyber-stalking arsonist intent on destroying lives?

In my twenty years on the force, I'd learned to recognize patterns obsessive stalkers followed. Their behavior typically escalated from minor disturbances to threats, arson, physical violence, and sometimes even murder. Christina didn't fit that pattern—not even close.

I flipped through her file again, searching desperately for something I'd overlooked. Her digital history before she went missing was mundane: online shopping, casual social media interactions, routine emails from work. Nothing hinted at advanced technological skills or suggested she could mastermind complex cyber-attacks. Her greatest technical talent seemed to be her proficiency in Excel—a far cry from the sophisticated digital torment Ethan Hall and Jade Sommer had endured.

The fire chief had confirmed the arson at Jade's house, noting gasoline had been used, making Christina's movements that night nearly impossible to track. There were over thirteen thousand gas stations in the state.

I'd even enlisted the help of the FBI and the US Marshals, yet Christina remained elusive. Nothing about her background suggested someone capable of vanishing while launching relentless attacks from the shadows.

Leaning back in my chair, I stared at the ceiling, recalling previous investigations. None matched the meticulous execution of this digital sabotage. The Christina described by her family and coworkers was kind and dependable, a woman who, when struggling with mental health, sought refuge—not revenge—in meditation centers or monasteries.

"Detective?"

The voice startled me from my thoughts. Seth Wellsey stood in the doorway, his lanky frame leaning casually against the jamb. At thirty-six, Seth was the department's top cyber-crime investigator. Dark-rimmed glasses perched on his nose, pale skin hinted at long hours spent indoors, and his thinning black hair was cropped neatly. He was one of the smartest people I knew, and I trusted his instincts implicitly.

"Please tell me you've got something, Seth," I said hopefully.

He sighed, stepping into my office and sinking into the chair across from me. "Wish I did. We're still going through a lot of data. Eventually, everyone makes a mistake, and we can hone in on them. It just takes time. Whoever's behind these attacks is good—really good," Seth said.

"You're doubting it's Christina?" I asked sharply.

He shrugged. "I've traced proxy servers, burner phones, fake accounts—everything," Seth said, his frustration clear. "I was able to track down one of the phones used, but they used cryptocurrency and the dark web. It's meticulous, technical, and completely clean. Either Christina suddenly became a world-class hacker overnight, or—"

"Or someone else is involved," I finished, feeling my pulse quicken.

He nodded slowly. "Exactly. First-timers always leave digital fingerprints—mistakes, a learning curve. There's none of that here. If your accountant really were behind this, we'd have found her by now."

My mind raced. If Christina wasn't responsible, then who was? The only other person in this tangled case with clear technological expertise was Ethan Hall—but that didn't add up either.

"We need to broaden our perspective," I said. "Let's reexamine everyone involved—Ethan, his ex-wife Kayla, Jade, even Dana Garza. We need to zoom out."

"It'll slow us down," he said with a sigh, "but I think you're right. It's the smartest move at this point."

"I want Ethan at the top of our list."

Seth looked at me sharply, eyebrows knitting together in confusion. "Why Ethan?"

"Because out of everyone entangled in this mess, Ethan is the only one with a documented IT background. He'd know how to hide digital footprints, set up proxies, burner accounts—all the things we've seen."

"Fair enough. He does have the skills, but do you really think he's capable of all this?"

"I don't know," I admitted, rubbing my temples as tension tightened across my forehead. "But we can't afford to overlook anyone."

A silence stretched between us before I spoke again, lowering my voice slightly. "I also want to take a closer look at the kid."

His eyes widened. "Tyler? He's only eleven, Nora."

"I know, and it feels awful even considering him," I replied uneasily. "But we've seen younger perpetrators before. He spends nearly all his time glued to a screen, so he's comfortable with technology. If he's upset about his father dating other women, who knows what he might be capable of."

Seth looked skeptical but remained thoughtful. "You really think a kid could orchestrate something this sophisticated?"

"It's unlikely. But that doesn't mean it's impossible. Let's not rule him out just yet. If we're zooming out, we need to be thorough—no exceptions."

"Understood. I'll cast a wider net. And I'll keep digging on Christina, too. We still can't afford to dismiss her entirely."

"Good," I said firmly, leaning back and feeling the

chair creak beneath my weight. "We need answers quickly."

Seth stood up, stretching his lanky frame. "I'll get started right away."

As he left the room, the realization hit me hard—I had fallen victim to tunnel vision, fixated solely on Christina Garza while ignoring other possibilities. What if Christina herself was a victim, manipulated by someone far more cunning and ruthless?

I shuddered at the thought, resolving to meticulously revisit every shred of evidence. Christina Garza was either a criminal mastermind, the likes of which I'd never encountered, or she was an unfortunate pawn, trapped in a web spun by someone far more dangerous.

It was time to widen the angle. The truth was out there, hidden within the details we'd overlooked. I just hoped we'd find it before someone else got hurt—or worse.

TWENTY-EIGHT
ETHAN

I was driving back to my apartment from Kayla's house. Despite everything going on, I felt happier than I had since this ordeal had begun. The last few hours I'd spent with Kayla and Tyler had been bliss. We were like a real family under the same roof again. I knew it was an illusion. But it was a pleasant fantasy to have as I made my way back to town towards my apartment.

I couldn't read her very well, but I could swear that Kayla had also had a good time, enjoying me hanging out with them. Kayla, of course, was still concerned about Tyler's safety, but she had taken the news about the video and me losing my job better than I'd thought. And had even made fun of the embarrassing sex tape video with me in it floating out there on the internet.

When I got up to leave, I almost headed upstairs to the bedroom, before remembering this wasn't my house. It was Kayla's, and we were divorced. I regretted not fighting harder for my marriage. I knew she was unhappy, but instead of trying to work at it and make changes, I just agreed to the divorce when she brought it up the first time. I just gave up. I don't know if it would have made a difference, but at least I would have tried, and I regretted not doing that.

I parked and trudged up to my apartment, exhaustion pulling at every limb. As I closed the door behind me, my phone buzzed in my pocket, startling me. It was past 10:30 at night, and I was filled with a sinking dread because I knew who was sending me a text message this late.

The screen showed me an image of Kayla, clearly taken without her knowledge. She was wearing her blue scrubs, stepping out of her car in the farmhouse's driveway. The photograph was dimly lit and grainy, but there was no mistaking it was her. My pulse roared in my ears.

A second text appeared beneath the photo:
It's always been about her, hasn't it?

The phone shook slightly in my trembling hands. Christina had once again found the perfect weapon, striking deep into the heart of my fears. She was no longer just targeting me and Jade—she had brought Kayla into her twisted game. Kayla, who'd done nothing wrong except marry me years ago.

How long had Christina been following her? Was Tyler safe? My mind raced with increasingly frantic questions, each more terrifying than the last. The helplessness was suffocating.

I dialed Kayla's number without thinking. The phone rang once, twice. "Hello? Ethan?" Kayla sounded calm, almost sleepy. She was probably getting ready for bed. A wave of relief washed through me just hearing her voice and knowing that she was all right.

"Kayla, are you okay?" My words stumbled out in a rush.

"Ethan, what's wrong? You just left half an hour ago."

"Has anything weird happened tonight? Did you notice anyone following you or anything strange?" I asked, struggling to keep calm.

She paused, clearly alarmed. "No. Why? Ethan, you're scaring me."

"Christina just sent me a photo of you at your house," I blurted. "You were in your work scrubs, so it wasn't taken tonight. But she's clearly been watching you."

"Oh my God," Kayla whispered. "You don't think she'd actually try to hurt me? Or Tyler?"

"I don't know. She's clearly dangerous. I'm coming back over—"

"No, Ethan." Kayla's resolve pushed past the fear. "It seems like you're being here tonight triggered her. She's obviously watching you too. You coming back here might escalate things. I'll call the police and let them handle this."

"The police haven't been able to catch her!" I snapped harshly, my panic turning into frustration. Immediately, regret washed over me. "I'm sorry. I didn't mean—"

Kayla sighed softly. "I know you're worried, Ethan. So am I. But Tyler's asleep. The doors are locked, and I'll get my grandfather's shotgun from the basement. We'll be okay."

I blinked, surprised. Kayla hated guns. She was so upset when I bought my handgun. But fear could change anyone's principles. Though that old shotgun was ancient—fifty or sixty years old—it might do more harm than good. Still, just having it might scare Christina away if worst came to worst.

"You should call the police," Kayla said. "Send whatever Christina sent you to the detective."

She was right, but doing nothing felt impossible. "Okay," I finally said, feeling defeated. "But promise me you'll call the police too immediately after we hang up. Text me if anything seems off."

"I promise," Kayla said gently. "And Ethan, you stay safe too."

After we hung up, every small noise—the hum of the refrigerator, a creak from the hallway—jolted my nerves.

With trembling fingers, I dialed the detective.

She answered promptly, her voice tense. "Galovich."

"Detective, it's Ethan Hall," I began.

"What's happened now?"

"Christina texted again. She's stalking Kayla too. She sent a photo of her outside her house," I said quickly, desperation creeping into my tone.

There was a momentary silence, then Galovich said, "Send me everything. I'll dispatch a unit to Kayla's immediately. We'll keep an eye out."

Some of my tension eased. "Thank you."

I forwarded the texts and photo to the detective, then stared out through the narrow slit between my drawn blinds. All I could see was the darkness of the night. I felt a chill knowing that Christina was out there, somewhere, hiding in plain sight.

And the police seemed incapable of finding her.

TWENTY-NINE
ETHAN

I HAD ANOTHER RESTLESS NIGHT BUT WAS relieved that Christina didn't show up to do something to Kayla and Tyler. I was terrified she might set the farmhouse on fire like she had done to Jade's house, but thankfully she tried nothing. She didn't harass me much over the next few days. I welcome the respite from her unrelenting abuse.

Over that time, the police finally seemed to kick their investigation into high gear, throwing more resources and manpower toward finding Christina. Search warrants were issued for Christina's and her mother's homes.

Kayla confirmed that a sheriff's deputy's patrol car had been regularly driving by to check on her and Tyler. I had even noticed a police cruiser driving past my apartment complex several times, and Detective

Galovich assured me they had investigators actively tracking down every lead, digital and otherwise.

Yet, despite the added scrutiny, Christina remained a ghost. No sightings, no tangible leads. It again seemed to me that Greenwood County Sheriff's Department was out of its league in this type of investigation.

The media had latched on to this sordid tale of online dating, stalking, arson, and twisted love triangles. Now it wasn't just the local crime beat reporters from The North Coast Examiner loitering around; a reporter from San Francisco ambushed me on the street, eager for an interview. I told him firmly I wasn't interested, but he persisted, shoving an iPhone toward me and peppering me with invasive questions until I climbed into my car and sped away, feeling like a low-budget celebrity dodging the paparazzi.

My embarrassment only deepened when an old friend from Los Angeles reached out, saying he'd read about the whole messy ordeal online. My life had become entertainment for the masses, the scandal spreading faster than I'd feared. It felt like a ticking time bomb—only a matter of time before national media picked up the scent, dragging my humiliation into the spotlight on an even bigger stage.

I dreaded telling my sister in Arizona. Our conversations were rare and typically superficial, limited to exchanging polite updates via occasional text messages. How could I even begin to explain this disaster to her?

Just the thought of broaching the subject left me nauseous.

And then there was the video—the intensely personal, utterly humiliating sex tape of Jade and me, now circulating freely in public view. The damage extended well beyond my former workplace; it had quickly made the rounds on social media and seedier corners of the internet. I'd become depressingly adept at filing DMCA claims, frantically trying to stem the tide. But each takedown triggered new uploads, multiplying faster than I could manage—an infuriating, relentless game of digital whack-a-mole against faceless voyeurs.

I couldn't bear to check the dark web, certain my disgrace had seeped into that lawless abyss. The ultimate invasion of privacy had even infiltrated YouTube. Despite the platform's strict guidelines against sexual content, among the three million videos uploaded daily—about 2,500 every minute—my humiliation occasionally slipped through. Sometimes those uploads lingered for hours or even days before moderators finally intervened.

It felt like drowning, and the shore was nowhere in sight.

I couldn't even summon the courage to begin a new job search, knowing the first thing prospective employers would do was Google my name—and the results were damning. Who would take a chance on someone tangled up with a deranged stalker like

Christina? Why would any company risk becoming her next target? Unemployment checks kept me afloat, but they were a fraction of what I'd earned at Fitzek—over sixty percent less than my previous take-home pay. Thankfully, I hadn't needed to tap into my savings yet, but I tightened my spending dramatically. If it hadn't been for Kayla regularly inviting me over for home-cooked meals, my diet would have consisted mostly of ramen noodles with the occasional splurge at Taco Bell.

Still, I tried to reclaim some normalcy in my life, despite the ongoing harassment. Ironically, amid all this chaos, Kayla and I had grown closer. We'd started spending more time together, dinners at her place, weekend afternoons in the backyard with Tyler. Our conversations flowed easily, the way they had when we were first together, and for brief moments it almost felt like we were a family again.

But Kayla remained firm: Tyler couldn't sleep at my apartment, not with Christina still on the loose. I agreed wholeheartedly. Tyler's safety was paramount, and if I had to sacrifice my nights alone at my place, it was a small price to pay. Instead, I spent as much time as I could with both at Kayla's, savoring the unexpected silver lining of reconnecting with my family.

Yet Christina's shadow still loomed over us. The digital harassment hadn't eased up—it had intensified. Not just me and Jade anymore; Kayla was now firmly in Christina's crosshairs. She received messages and photographs of herself at the hospital, at the grocery store, even picking Tyler up from school. It terrified me, knowing Christina had been watching her.

At Detective Galovich's urging, Kayla went to court to file a restraining order against Christina, just as I had done the week before. Mine was classified as a domestic violence restraining order due to our prior intimacy, while Jade and Kayla's were civil harassment orders. Yet, as I filled out the paperwork, I couldn't shake a cynical sense of futility about the entire process.

"Is this even worth it?" I asked Galovich bluntly, signing the final document. "Nobody's seen Christina in two months. Do you honestly think a piece of paper will stop her? What if it just makes things worse?"

Galovich's eyes met mine steadily, her expression firm yet empathetic. "I understand your frustration, Ethan, but this is another tool at our disposal. The moment she violates this, we have immediate grounds to arrest her."

"You'd have to find her first," I snapped, unable to mask the bitterness and exhaustion that had built up inside me.

Her jaw tightened slightly. "We'll find whoever is behind this, Ethan. I promise you."

I hoped her confidence wasn't misplaced. But something about the subtle shift in her wording nagged at me—her repeated use of phrases like "whoever" or "the person responsible." Was it simply standard police caution, or did it hint at something else? Who else but Christina could be behind all this? The way Galovich had watched me, her eyes lingering a little longer than usual, filled me with unease. I reminded myself that cops were suspicious by nature. Yet I couldn't shake the uncomfortable feeling that since the cops could not find her, suspicion might soon fall on someone other than Christina—perhaps even me. I told myself I was being paranoid.

Later that evening, sitting on Kayla's porch, I finally felt a brief respite from the relentless anxiety. Tyler curled up next to me on the wooden swing, his head resting gently against my shoulder. The rhythmic creak of the swing matched our breathing, slow and steady. Kayla stepped out onto the porch, handing me a steaming cup of coffee. She offered a small, reassuring smile as she sat down beside us.

"We'll get through this, Ethan," she whispered.

I desperately wanted to believe her, but I knew this living nightmare we were all part of was far from over.

THIRTY
ETHAN

I agreed to meet Jade at North Coast Jitters, a small coffee shop just off Main Street in downtown Fairdale.

When she asked to see me, I was surprised. I hadn't seen her since our awkward parting after her house fire. Once she'd moved into her mountain property miles from town, our interactions had become limited to brief business-like texts, mostly concerning requests from Detective Galovich for information or minor details to aid their investigation.

Everything that had happened to her because of Christina, because of me, made me feel terribly guilty, so the least I could do was to meet her for a coffee.

I arrived first, ordering a plain black coffee and grabbing a table by the window. Minutes later, Jade stepped in, and my heart gave an unexpected lurch. She looked different somehow. Her face was thinner, her usually vibrant eyes seemed duller, and a hint of sadness clung to her expression. I supposed Christina had that effect on all of us.

"Hey," she said softly.

"Hey," I replied, trying to sound casual, though my nerves were jumping. She excused herself to order a drink. I heard her ordering her usual, a Caramel Macchiato.

She returned to the table, sliding into the seat across from me.

"How have you been?" I asked.

She shrugged slightly, forcing a small smile. "Fine, I suppose. It's good to see you, Ethan."

That took me by surprise, but I forced myself to smile back. "You too."

We sat in uncomfortable silence for a moment, each unsure of how to begin. Finally, Jade broke the awkwardness. "I've missed you," she said, her voice quiet, almost meek, which was quite the contrast to her usual bravado.

I shifted uncomfortably in the chair. I hadn't been fair, using her for my comfort when convenient then pushing her away when things got complicated. "Jade, I—"

She raised a hand, cutting me off gently. "It's okay. You don't have to say anything. I know where things stand between us. I just wanted to see you. Even if it is just for a few minutes."

Her understanding somehow made me feel worse.

I cleared my throat, searching for something neutral to say. "How's your place up the mountain treating you?"

She shrugged, offering a thin smile. "It's smaller than my house. But it's quiet. Peaceful. Good for clearing my head."

"Sounds nice," I replied, fumbling for words. It felt surreal, the distance between us now, the emotional canyon carved by everything Christina had put us through. The coffee shop buzzed around us, patrons laughing, enjoying pastries, oblivious to the strained tension at our little corner table.

When they called her name for the drink, I quickly stood. "I'll get it." It was not as much me being a gentleman as me needing to get some air, even if just by walking up to the counter and back.

She smiled and thanked me when I brought her order back to her.

Jade stared down into her coffee cup, swirling it slowly. "So, any news from the detective?"

I sighed, relieved she'd steered the conversation toward safer territory. "No. Nothing new. They're still chasing shadows. Christina seems to have vanished. Yet she's everywhere. I'm not too confident in the Greenwood Sheriff's department skills at the moment."

Jade nodded her head. "I just don't understand how she can keep hiding like this. They're like the Keystone cops chasing their tails while she runs around with impunity."

"It's surreal," I said, frustration clear in my voice.

"But Detective Galovich seems very confident they're getting closer to catching her. They took a bunch of things from me to search," I said, trying to sound optimistic about their current lack of progress.

Jade seemed surprised as she took a sip of her coffee, eyes downcast. "Really? What did they take?"

"Mostly electronic devices. I had a box full of them. I'm a bit of a device hoarder. Even though some were from before I moved here, even my old Blackberry, the police wanted them all so they could look through them. I figured what the hell and gave it to them. How about you? Have they asked for your devices?"

"Detective Galovich has called me, but I've been busy on a couple house flips in Eureka, and up at my new place. Plus, meeting with my architect to rebuild my house, I've been too busy. Besides, all my stuff burned down in my house, so I don't really have anything to give them."

"I never imagined she could do something so terrible," I managed to say.

"I guess love makes people do crazy things," she said.

"What she did goes way beyond that. I hope that when they do catch her, they put her away for some serious prison time."

She looked at me intently as she sipped her drink. "So, how are things with Kayla?"

That change of topic caught me off guard. I didn't

feel comfortable talking about my ex-wife with a girl I had dated. It took me a moment to think it over. I stumbled over my response. "Um, well. We're good, I guess. We've been spending a lot of time together lately. It's almost like um—" I caught myself, heat rising to my face as I quickly corrected, "I mean, mostly I'm spending time at her place with Tyler. We're trying to shield him from what's going on."

She raised an eyebrow, clearly not convinced. "Right. For Tyler," she said slowly.

I nodded quickly, uncomfortable with the implication hanging in the air. The silence stretched between us again, heavier than before. But I didn't respond, just sat there quietly, feeling very uncomfortable.

"Anyway," Jade said finally, her voice carefully neutral. "I appreciate you meeting me today. I just wanted to check in."

Relieved that the meeting was drawing to a close, I said, mostly lying, "Yeah, thanks for calling. It was nice to catch up."

We stood up and exchanged a brief, awkward hug, then I headed for the door. I didn't look back, but I could feel her watching me leave.

THIRTY-ONE
JADE

He was so full of shit. I know he didn't enjoy meeting me here to catch up. He was just being polite. But I just smiled after the ice-cold hug he gave me.

I watched Ethan leave the coffee shop, a knot tightening painfully in my stomach. I didn't know what I expected from him. Part of me wanted to be angry, to lash out at his endless indecision, but mostly I just felt hurt. The ache of rejection lingered, heavy and persistent, mingled with the sting of embarrassment. How had I allowed myself to become this vulnerable, this exposed?

Slowly, I sank back into my seat, fingertips tapping restlessly against the cool tabletop, my drink long since gone cold. Through the window, I followed Ethan's retreating figure until he disappeared around the corner, bitterness surging anew in my chest—a familiar, unwelcome feeling. The humiliation of needing him—

of wanting him so badly—made my skin burn with shame.

Worse was how he lit up talking about Kayla. I'm sure he wasn't even aware of it. The softness in his eyes whenever he spoke her name felt like the deepest betrayal, sharper than any other. It was a tenderness he'd never shown me, not even in our most intimate moments. Had I really been nothing more than a convenient distraction? A temporary fix until he could win back the woman he truly wanted?

All his bullshit about casual dating—he'd just wanted someone to fill the void, someone disposable. I might as well be a sex doll.

It was obvious he still pined for Kayla, the woman who'd divorced him and moved 700 miles away. And he'd come all the way up here, trailing after her like a lost puppy. And I was the one who couldn't move on? He had never gotten over her. How could I have been so stupid?

I shut my eyes briefly, fighting back the painful truth I'd known deep down for weeks. Ethan would never choose me—or Christina, or anyone else. It had always been Kayla. She occupied that special place in his heart, and nothing I did would ever change that.

"Everything okay, hon?" The waitress's gentle voice snapped me from my spiraling thoughts. She'd worked here most of her life, always quick with a smile and a joke. Now she watched me sympathetically as she cleared our empty coffee cups from the table.

"I'm fine, Polly," I lied, forcing a weary smile. "Just lost in thought."

She nodded with the look of someone who'd heard this story a thousand times and walked back toward the kitchen, leaving me alone with my humiliation. Outside, the street was quiet, deceptively peaceful, yet every inch felt tainted with memories of Ethan. I could still smell his cologne in the air. I took a deep breath. And I slowly let it out. I felt like I was expunging him from my body.

It was at that moment that something shifted within me. I was tired—so unbelievably tired—of clinging to false hope, of letting him hold this power over me. I needed to reclaim my dignity. Fairdale had become nothing but a reminder of my humiliation and pain. The charred ruins of my house stood as a stark symbol of my shattered relationship with Ethan. Rebuilding it—brick by brick, plank by plank—might offer me the chance to regain control, to heal the wounds Ethan had left. Once I had a new house built, I would flip it. I was done with Fairdale.

Resolve slowly replaced despair. Yes, that was exactly what I'd do. I'd rebuild, make the house perfect, flip it quickly, and finally leave this town and Ethan in it forever. It was time to close this painful chapter and start fresh, far from Fairdale and its tangled memories.

Leaving a tip on the table, I slipped on my coat and stepped out into the brisk air, my footsteps feeling lighter already. A newfound determination guided me forward.

By the time I reached my car, my mind was set. But a stubborn thought nagged at me: Why should I let myself be chased away like this? I wasn't a quitter. Never had been. Why start now? I'd fought my entire life—from foster home to foster home, through bruises, abuse, and neglect. I'd survived horrors most couldn't imagine. None of those bastards had ever broken me down completely. I wasn't about to let anyone take that strength from me.

THIRTY-TWO
ETHAN

That evening, I went over to Kayla's house again. Tyler was ecstatic to see me, immediately diving into an animated, intricate explanation of a new video game he'd mastered. Watching him describe it with vivid gestures and bright, excited eyes made me momentarily forget the storm swirling around our lives. Kayla and I had done our best to shield him, and it filled me with relief and pride to see our efforts paying off.

Kayla had prepared her famous homemade lasagna, rich and bubbling with golden melted cheese on top, accompanied by slices of warm garlic bread. I'd brought a Caesar salad, though admittedly I'd cheated, grabbing one of those pre-packaged kits from the grocery store. Kayla didn't seem to mind, offering me a soft smile as she took the bowl from my hands and set it on the table.

She opened a bottle of red wine, pouring two generous glasses for us and apple juice for Tyler.

"Cheers," she said softly, raising her glass. Her eyes met mine, the warmth in them causing my pulse to quicken.

"To peace and quiet," I responded, gently clinking my glass against hers. But even now, relaxing as this felt, my eyes kept drifting toward the windows, alert for any sign of trouble, any sign of *her*. Even when she wasn't bombarding me with threats, Christina was always on my mind.

After dinner, we let Tyler play a bit longer, but around nine Kayla nudged him gently. He protested with mild reluctance, yawning even as he tried to bargain for more time. Eventually, he gave up, trudging toward the stairs with exaggerated slowness.

"Goodnight, sweetheart," Kayla called, her voice tender and soothing.

"Night, Dad," Tyler added, glancing back over his shoulder with a sleepy smile.

"Sleep tight," I replied, feeling a warmth spread through me.

Once Tyler was safely upstairs, Kayla refilled our glasses, emptying the first bottle of wine. Without hesitation, she reached for a second bottle, uncorked it, and poured generously.

We settled on the couch, the distance between us gradually closing as we reminisced about simpler times —holidays spent together, road trips full of mishaps, silly family traditions we'd once shared. Laughter flowed naturally, like water finding its familiar path, but we carefully skirted around anything painful: our divorce, Christina, the media circus that had invaded our lives.

By midnight, the two bottles of wine had worked their magic, the room around us warm and pleasantly spinning. Kayla leaned closer, placing a gentle hand on my knee. Her touch sent electricity through me, and for a heartbeat, the world seemed to pause. I waited, breathlessly wondering if she might invite me up to her room.

"You can't drive home like this," she finally said, her voice soft, slightly slurred from the wine. "Stay here tonight."

"Sure," I said, careful not to betray my eager hope.

She stood slowly. For one long moment, she looked down at me, a question forming on her lips, an invitation perhaps. But then, with a slight shake of her head —as if reminding herself of boundaries—she gave me a shy smile instead.

"The guest room down the hall is ready for you. Fresh sheets and towels."

"Of course," I said, masking my disappointment. My heart sank, even as understanding settled in its place.

She lingered briefly then turned away and ascended the stairs without another word.

Once in the lonely room, I fell on the guest bed and

stared at the ceiling, my mind spinning—not just from the wine, but from the anticipation and frustration mingling throughout my body.

Sleep came reluctantly. When it did, it dragged along into a nightmare. I saw Christina, her figure shadowy and menacing, silently climbing the stairs towards Tyler's room. Her footsteps were quiet, methodical, those of a predator stalking her prey. My heart raced as I struggled to move, but my limbs felt weighted, useless. In the dream, I tried shouting Tyler's name to warn him, but no sound escaped my throat. She turned towards me and gave me an evil smirk as she went into Tyler's room and slammed the door shut.

I woke suddenly, drenched in sweat, heart pounding. Sitting up quickly, I fought to catch my breath. The nightmare felt disturbingly real.

Unable to shake the dread, I padded quietly up the stairs to Tyler's room. The door was ajar. Inside, Tyler was sprawled across his bed, breathing deeply. His laptop was tossed carelessly beside him, the screen darkened. Seeing him safe allowed me to exhale deeply, though I was still worried about how much time he spent online. It was a generational thing; I supposed Generation Alpha—the first to be born entirely in the 21st century and the third millennium—practically lived online. I had driven carpool with Tyler and his friends in the backseat, the three boys texting each other and giggling instead of just putting the phones away and talking. I'd wanted to wait another year or two before letting Tyler have a phone, but I lost that battle.

I moved the laptop to the desk, pulling the covers over Tyler before silently stepping back out.

THE NEXT MORNING, the three of us ate breakfast in the sunlit kitchen; scrambled eggs and turkey sausage links filled the room with familiar, comforting scents. Tyler pushed eggs around on his plate, looking thoughtful.

"Are you guys back together now?" he asked suddenly, eyes flicking innocently between us.

Kayla choked on her coffee, sputtering. I flushed. We glanced at each other, embarrassed and caught off guard.

"No, Tyler," Kayla explained softly, recovering first. "We're not back together, but we'll always both be here for you, okay? That'll never change, no matter what happens between your dad and me."

I nodded quickly, echoing her sentiment. "We both love you very much, buddy."

Tyler shrugged nonchalantly, obviously not fully grasping the weight of his question. "Okay, can I go now?"

Kayla sighed once Tyler had gone upstairs, clearly uncomfortable. "We're confusing him, Ethan. Last night was probably a mistake."

"It's not a big deal," I insisted, though I felt stung.

"It was safer, with everything going on. I felt better being here, keeping an eye on things."

"Maybe, but it's too soon. He's still processing the divorce, and spending nights here together, having dinner, drinking wine—it's sending Tyler mixed signals. We can't do that to him. So we need to cool things off between us."

I bit back my irritation, realizing with a pang how similar her tone sounded to the speech I'd given Jade and Christina. Being on the receiving end felt awful. I needed to go. "You're probably right. I'll head home."

I hugged Tyler goodbye and drove back to my apartment, feeling defeated.

Once home, I stood in a hot shower, letting the water run over me until my frustration began to fade. Was it so bad that we were spending time as a family? Even though we were divorced, we shared a child, so like it or not, we were stuck together for life.

Afterwards, still damp, I checked my phone. A notification caught my attention immediately, coming from yet another unfamiliar international number—this one with a country code I didn't even recognize.

It was Christina.

You spent the night fucking Kayla. Congrats. But just remember. You can't always have everything going your way.

THIRTY-THREE
ETHAN

I don't know how long I stood there, staring numbly at Christina's latest threat displayed cruelly on my phone's screen. The dull throb behind my eyes immediately intensified into a sharp ache. My grip tightened around the device, knuckles whitening. How long could this possibly go on? How many nights would I spend trapped in this relentless nightmare?

I was already spiraling, frustration and anxiety tangled together after the earlier conversation about Kayla not wanting to spend more time with me. Now Christina's poisonous message threatened to push me over the edge.

My thumb hovered over the keyboard in an instinctive urge to fire back, a reply surging through me. I typed quickly: *Nothing happened. I slept alone in the guest room.* Then, just as quickly, I deleted it. Engaging would only feed her obsession, draw me deeper into her twisted game.

But silence hadn't worked either. For weeks, I'd absorbed her vile messages without responding. I was tired of playing passive victim, tired of turning the other cheek and waiting helplessly for her next attack.

With a heavy sigh, I forwarded the message to Detective Galovich, not even bothering to add my usual frustrated commentary. She damned well knew who sent this. I had lost faith in the detective and the entire Greenwood County Sheriff's Department. Each threat seemed to push Christina further beyond their reach, leaving me to fend for myself.

My apartment suddenly felt claustrophobic. I paced restlessly, anxiety buzzing beneath my skin. I needed to get out, clear my head. It was early in the evening, desperate for distraction, I grabbed my keys and headed out the door.

Fifteen minutes later, I stepped inside Bigfoot's. I didn't know if I was half hoping or half fearing I'd see Jade. Images of our nights together here flooded me briefly, only to be extinguished instantly by humiliating memories of our leaked sex tape. The thought made my stomach churn. When I spoke to anyone, I wondered: Did they watch it?

"She's not here," the bartender said curtly as our eyes met, his tone dripping with accusation. "Hasn't been around in weeks."

I nodded awkwardly, embarrassed, and ordered a

beer, retreating quickly to the back corner. I busied myself with darts, trying to drown my thoughts with the mechanical repetition of throwing and retrieving, punctuated by occasional sips of beer.

Halfway through my second beer, one of the regulars approached. I'd seen her before but never spoken to her—a petite woman with wavy blond hair and a friendly smile. We exchanged small talk and laughs, and played a few rounds of darts which distracted me momentarily from the storm inside my head.

For a fleeting moment, driven by loneliness and sheer frustration, I considered making a move. Her lingering smile, subtle eyebrow raises, and playful glances hinted she might be open to it, but then I felt a fresh surge of guilt and caution. The last thing I needed was to pull someone else into Christina's twisted sights.

"It's getting late," I finally said, stepping back politely. "Thanks for the game."

She smiled, looking slightly disappointed, but didn't press. "Maybe next time."

OUTSIDE, the street was dark, illuminated by the glow of a few scattered streetlamps. It was just past ten as I walked toward my parked Jeep, half a block away.

I was pressing the FOB button to unlock the car when headlights flashed across my back. Initially, I paid it no mind, dismissing it as some driver passing through town too quickly. But the sound of the engine roaring closer, tires humming menacingly over the pavement, made me glance back.

My heart jolted. A dark car barreled toward me down Main Street, way too fast. My pulse surged violently as recognition struck—a gleaming BMW, the unmistakable logo flashing briefly under the glare of a streetlamp.

It veered suddenly, headlights locked on me, high beams flooding my vision. Fear paralyzed me for half a second before adrenaline kicked in. I threw an arm up to shield my eyes from the blinding LED lights as the vehicle sped toward me like a missile.

The engine's deafening roar filled my ears as I lunged forward, scrambling awkwardly onto my jeep's hood. I barely cleared the BMW's bumper as it slammed into the Jeep. The brutal crunch of metal and shattering glass filled the air as pain exploded through my hip. The impact flung me sideways, sending me crashing onto the pavement.

My shoulder scraped against rough asphalt as my breath was knocked from my lungs. For a terrifying second, my vision blurred into darkness, punctuated by dizzying flashes of white-hot agony. I gasped, clawing at the ground, willing my body to move.

Struggling to my feet, I leaned heavily against the passenger side of my Jeep, gasping for breath. My heart thundered, adrenaline drowning out the pain in my battered body. The BMW didn't pause. No screech of brakes, no hesitation. The car sped on, disappearing swiftly into the night, fading red taillights the only evidence of its brutal assault.

My breath came in ragged gasps, adrenaline still pounding. "Christina," I whispered bitterly. My hands shook. "Damn you."

Slowly, pain returned—sharp, fiery stabs radiating through my shoulder and hip. I limped around the Jeep, surveying the damage. The driver's side mirror lay shattered on the ground, bits of glass sparkling cruelly under the streetlamp. Deep gouges marred the side panel and door. My Jeep. I loved that car.

I was surprised no one was around. I expected people to come out and check on the commotion, but no one did. It made me wonder: Had she succeeded in killing me, how long would I lie dead in the street before someone found me? I'd never felt so alone. But I suppose that, aside from the bar, the other businesses had long ago closed for the day. I fumbled for my phone, fingers trembling, and dialed 911.

I looked around to make sure Christina wasn't coming back to finish me off, but the street remained deserted, as if nothing had happened. Just another quiet night in Fairdale.

THIRTY-FOUR
ETHAN

I sat on the cold examination table in the hospital's emergency room, shivering despite the warm air blowing steadily from the vents overhead. The thin hospital gown offered little comfort, and the sterile smell of antiseptics made my stomach churn. It was surreal to be back here, in the very place to which they'd rushed Jade after her house fire. Just weeks later, here I was again, a victim myself. Another physical victim of Christina's madness.

A nurse moved swiftly around me, checking vitals, jotting down notes, and asking brief clinical questions about my pain. The ER doctor, a woman in her late forties with tired eyes and a reassuring smile, pressed spots along my shoulder and hip, her gloved hands efficient but compassionate.

"We'll need some imaging," she said, stepping back and stripping off her gloves. "X-rays of your shoulder and hip. And given the nature of your accident, I'd like to order a CT scan of your head—just as a precaution."

Accident? What had happened to me was no accident, but I didn't say that.

"Is that necessary?" I asked, trying not to sound anxious.

"Better safe than sorry," she replied with a weary yet professional smile before she hurried off toward her next emergency.

I spent the next hour being wheeled back and forth between various rooms for scans and x-rays, each movement intensifying the ache in my body. When I finally returned to the ER bay, two uniformed officers waited—one a California Highway Patrol trooper, the other a deputy from the Greenwood County Sheriff's Department. They looked grim, ready to interrogate rather than comfort.

"Mr. Hall," the deputy began, his tone formal, almost detached, "we need your statement regarding tonight's hit-and-run incident."

"It was Christina Garza," I blurted, before he could even finish his sentence. "She tried to kill me. She's been stalking and harassing me for weeks."

The deputy exchanged a look with the trooper. "Did you see her behind the wheel?" the trooper asked, pen poised over his notepad.

"No," I admitted, frustrated. "It was dark, the headlights blinded me, and I was too busy diving out of the way to get a look at the driver. But I recognized the car immediately—a black BMW. Her car."

They wrote that down, but their expressions remained unreadable. They asked me to walk them through everything that had happened with Christina from the start. I looked at them with dismay. Forcing myself to go through each detail yet again only amplified my irritation and helplessness, so I tried to push back.

"Can't you get all this from Detective Galovich?" I finally asked with impatience. "She's handling the case."

"We're aware of Detective Galovich's investigation," the deputy responded calmly, clearly unfazed by my frustration. "But for our reports, we need to hear it directly from you."

With no other choice, I again recounted the last two months of my life—the stalking, the threats, the escalating danger. At every repeated detail, my agitation grew, along with my exhaustion.

Finally, after what felt like an eternity, they seemed satisfied. The trooper closed his notebook, and the deputy nodded sympathetically.

"We'll do everything we can to locate Ms. Garza," he assured me, but the words felt hollow, as I'd heard that from Detective Galovich over and over without seeing a resolution.

. . .

AFTER WAITING AROUND FOR AN HOUR, the doctor returned looking at the X-rays on the computer monitor and nodding in agreement even though we hadn't spoken, so I wasn't sure who she was agreeing with. Herself, I suppose.

"You're pretty banged up, but nothing's broken and no head injury," she said, carefully pressing around my hip. I winced. "Just bruised, which will heal with rest. Your shoulder, though—road rash. That'll sting for a few days. Keep it clean, keep applying the ointment we gave you, and you'll be fine. You can try over-the-counter pain relievers like acetaminophen or ibuprofen to manage pain and inflammation, along with applying ice and resting the hip. But you're a fortunate man, Mr. Hall. You'll be fine in a couple of weeks."

My injury was so minor, it didn't even merit stronger pain killers. I guess that was a good sign. Considering everything, I agreed with the doctor. I was lucky. I'd seen the mangled aftermath of hit-and-run accidents, and compared to what could've happened, I'd gotten off easy. A few scrapes, bruises, and a banged-up car—that was it.

The trooper had told me before he left that my car was damaged, but drivable. I remembered looking at it while I waited for the first responders to arrive after I called 911. The driver's side door and front panel bore deep scrapes, dents forming a jagged pattern like an angry scar. My side mirror was obliterated, its shattered pieces strewn across the pavement. It was a grim reminder of how close I'd come to something far worse.

After the doctor left, Detective Galovich walked in, accompanied by Deputy Rivera.

While the deputy asked basic questions about the incident, pen in hand, notebook flipped open, ready to jot down details for a report, Galovich stood quietly, observing me closely. But I had had enough. "I just went through all this with another deputy and a CHP trooper. Get the details from them. I'm going home," I said, not caring that I was being rude. I was done for the night. They seemed incapable of cracking this cursed case.

"It would just help to add the details from your accident to our case file," Rivera said.

"This wasn't an accident," I insisted in frustration. "It was Christina. I know it."

The deputy raised an eyebrow skeptically. "Did you see her? Get a good look at the driver?"

"I just went through all this. No, it happened so fast, and the headlights blinded me. But it was a BMW —the exact kind Christina drives," I argued, gripping the edge of the examination table.

He shrugged dismissively. "A lot of BMWs out there."

"Not in Fairdale," I shot back. "This is Ford F-Series and Dodge RAM country. BMWs are as rare as unicorns around here," I sighed loudly. "I'm done here.

I've been cleared to go home, and that's what I'm going to do."

The deputy exchanged an uncomfortable glance with Galovich before excusing himself, promising they'd be on the lookout for a damaged BMW. But I didn't have much faith they could find Christina's car either.

Once we were alone, Galovich pulled up a chair and sat down, studying me with concern.

"Hang in there, Ethan," she said softly. "Believe it or not, we're making progress."

"Progress? She just tried to kill me," I snapped. "And you cops don't even believe me because I didn't see her behind the wheel. But I know it was her."

"I believe you. It would be too much of a coincidence otherwise."

"Then why can't you find her—or the car?" I pressed.

"We're looking at security footage now. Unfortunately, Bigfoot's security camera is aimed at their front door, not the street. We only have shadows and passing lights. And we don't have any witnesses."

I shook my head, feeling utterly defeated. "So yet again, you have nothing."

"Not yet," she admitted reluctantly. "But we're still searching. We're going to find her."

I'd heard that before, but I kept that to myself. I'd lashed out enough to the main detective on the case.

Around two a.m., I left the hospital, exhaustion

and anger simmering inside me. By the time I got home, the fury had overtaken my fatigue. I would not be a sitting duck for her again. I knew exactly what I'd do if she came after me or, worse, Kayla and Tyler.

I moved straight to my bedroom closet to get my gun. If the police can't end this. I will. I opened the safe and couldn't believe what I saw.

THIRTY-FIVE
JADE

I left my place at dusk, my nerves on edge.

As I drove, my memories of everything that had happened between Ethan and me churned through my mind, restless and unrelenting. This relationship had consumed me. It's all I could think about and I just couldn't seem to shut those thoughts down. I couldn't walk away as easily as Ethan had seemed to have done. I felt warm.

I rolled down the windows. The mountain air grew cooler as my car climbed higher up the mountain, the twisted road carving through dense redwoods. The wind felt good against my skin. The scent of pine and wet earth filled my lungs. Each turn up the mountain felt more precarious than the last. A flimsy metal barrier barely separated me from the steep ravine beyond.

For a moment, I thought about swerving off the edge.

Peace. At last.

No. Not like that.

It took about ten minutes to drive up from my place which was located lower down the mountain—the one I'd been forced into after everything burned.

A second hand life after the house fire, patched together with scraps of what I used to have.

By the time I parked at the trailhead, twilight had taken hold. The forest was folding into darkness, the towering trees like silent sentinels. They had stood for centuries, bearing witness to countless secrets—and tonight, they would bear witness to mine.

I told myself Ethan might come. That he might still remember this place. Our place.

I had texted him. No reply.

He had ghosted me, just like before.

First Christina. Now Kayla.

Always someone else.

Never me.

The last sliver of sunlight dipped below the treetops. I caught my reflection in the rearview mirror—pale, expectant, almost fragile. My hair was wind-whipped. I smoothed it down, adjusted my jacket, my hands trembling slightly. From the cold—or from fear of what was about to happen?

Tonight was supposed to mean something.

It had to.

I couldn't keep carrying this weight.

Not alone.

I locked the car and slipped the keys into my pocket. His car wasn't in the lot. Not yet.

Maybe he had parked farther up the road. Maybe he was already waiting at the clearing, too nervous—or too guilty—to be seen.

The forest smelled of damp moss and something older, wilder. I clicked on my flashlight and started down the trail, my steps quick, heart hammering.

I ignored the faded sign warning visitors to stay on the main path. That had never stopped me before. Some rules weren't made for people like us.

The hidden trail was just as I remembered: overgrown but familiar, a narrow path flattened by years of stolen footsteps.

I wondered how many other couples had made their way down to the clearing to make love. Were they still together?

I pictured a happy couple at home somewhere—cozy, content, planning their future—and hated them with a bitterness that tightened my throat.

The clearing where we made love opened before me.

I paused at the edge, the beam of my flashlight sliced through the gloom.

The familiar hush of the forest pressed in, broken only by the occasional rustle of wind in the leaves.

"Ethan?" I called softly, my voice cracking with hope.

No response.

Only the low murmur of the trees settling into night.

I stepped deeper into the clearing, brushing past the ferns, the memories pressing in around me.

I could almost feel him here again—lying on the ground beside me, his body against mine, our warm breaths mingling in the cool air, our hips moving in perfect rhythm.

The memory made my skin tingle, my chest ache.

How could he not see it?

How could he not feel it, too?

For a moment—just a heartbeat—I thought I saw him. A dark figure at the edge of the clearing, standing motionless, watching me.

"Ethan?" I whispered, stepping forward.

But when I shined the flashlight toward it, there was nothing there. Only shadows twisting between the trees.

My breath hitched.

The bitter taste of disappointment flooded my mouth.

My breath came faster, ragged and broken.

Something inside me frayed, snapped loose.

I couldn't let it end like this.

I wouldn't.

A blur of anger, grief, and desperation surged through me—sharp, bright, final.

And then—

A sudden flash.

A deafening crack shattered the stillness of the evening echoing off the trees.

A firestorm of pain ripped through my side, stealing the breath from my lungs.

I gasped, staggering back.

I looked down. Blood poured hot between my fingers as I clutched my side.

My knees buckled—but somehow, I stayed upright.

I ran.

Branches whipped my face as I scrambled up the path, the ground pitching beneath my frantic steps. Every breath was a battle against the agony lancing through my ribs.

My hands fumbled for my phone, slick with blood, my vision swimming.

"Help," I croaked into the darkness.

No signal at first.

Then—bars. Weak, but enough.

I stabbed at the screen, somehow dialing 911.

"911, what's your emergency?" a calm voice crackled through the speaker.

"I've been shot," I gasped, collapsing onto the dirt trail. "Please help me. I'm at Redwood Grove Trail... Whitehall Park... Please hurry!"

The operator's voice became a distant hum in my

ear, slipping further away with each beat of my struggling heart.

The 911 operator asked me questions but I could barely speak as I stumbled onto the parking lot, dragging myself forward on shaking legs.

The phone slipped from my fingers.

My head lolled against the cold asphalt, the world narrowing to a dark, endless tunnel.

Somewhere in the fog, I pictured Ethan—rushing to my side, his face full of regret, reaching out for me at last.

Maybe now he'd understand.

Maybe now he'd finally realize we belonged together.

With Kayla out of the way.

THIRTY-SIX
JADE

I woke up groggy and disoriented. It took me a moment to realize where I was—the pale blue walls, the soft beep of monitors, and the dull ache in my side reminded me I was in a hospital. Slowly, my eyes adjusted to the bright sunlight streaming through the blinds.

A nurse noticed me stirring and quickly stepped over, checking the monitors and gently adjusting the IV line.

"How are you feeling, Jade?" she asked kindly, jotting down notes on a clipboard.

"I don't know," I murmured, touching the tender area at my side. "How bad is it?"

She offered a reassuring smile. "You're very lucky. The bullet grazed you; it's superficial. The doctor will be in shortly, but I believe they're preparing your discharge papers."

I frowned, puzzled. It had felt much worse last night, or at least that's how I remembered it. I recalled the sharp, burning sensation, the frantic dash through the woods, and the terrifying phone call to 911. I shuddered, remembering the fear I'd felt. Yet now, in the clarity of the morning, the wound seemed almost trivial compared to the memory of the attack. But I was relieved it wasn't more serious. I looked around, hoping to see Ethan rush to my side like he had on the night of the fire, but he wasn't there.

"Thank you," I said to the nurse, and laid back against the pillow.

A few moments later I heard a gentle knock on the door. I sat up, hoping to see Ethan, but it wasn't him. It was Detective Galovich who appeared in the doorway, her face unreadable but her eyes sharp and inquisitive.

"Jade," she said calmly, stepping into the room, pulling a chair up next to the bed. "Glad to see you're awake. How are you holding up?"

"I'm okay, I guess. They said it wasn't serious."

"You got lucky," she agreed, studying me closely. "But we need to talk about last night. Tell me what happened."

I hesitated, looking away. "I...I'm not sure exactly. It was dark. I thought I was meeting Ethan—"

"Ethan Hall?" she asked quickly.

"Yes," I admitted, flushing.

"Ethan Hall asked you to meet him out in the woods at night, and you agreed?"

I didn't like the judgment in her tone. She made me feel stupid. Hard up.

"I asked him. We went there when we were dating. It was our spot. Outdoors. And I'm not talking about camping."

"I understand," Galovich said, frowning at me, scribbling in her notepad.

I had always been forthcoming about my sexuality. I wouldn't let anyone slut-shame me. What was the big deal? Sex was normal. Men turned it into something shameful to control us. And yet, it was other women, like Detective Nora Galovich, the way she was looking down at me at that moment, who judged other women the most.

She looked up from her notepad. "What happened next?"

"When I got there, someone else was waiting for me. I couldn't see clearly. It was dark."

"But you're sure it wasn't Ethan?"

"No. It wasn't Ethan," I said defensively. By the look on the detective's face, I might have been too defensive.

"How can you be so sure? You said it was dark and you couldn't see who shot you. So it could have been Ethan, then, right?" Galovich asked. I didn't like how she was looking at me. It was a smug look that pissed me off. I wanted to slap the smugness from her face. My fists balled up under the sheets.

I sat up from the bed. My body was tense. My side

ached from the gunshot wound, but I ignored it. "It wasn't Ethan. I told you, he wasn't there!"

"But you know who shot you. Don't you?"

I felt my body shrink back down as the adrenaline of my anger left me. I slid back down into the bed.

"No," I said, looking out the window.

Galovich leaned forward. "You said something specific to the 911 dispatcher. I've listened to the recording several times. I have the transcript right here. You said, 'the bitch shot me.' You said, 'she.' So I know you saw who shot you, didn't you, Jade?"

Why was she asking about Ethan then? I hated how the cops played head games all the time.

"I was scared. Maybe I assumed..."

"No," Galovich cut in. "I've been a cop for a long time, Jade. People don't say something like that unless they have a pretty good idea who attacked them. Why are you protecting the person that shot you?"

I stared down at the sheets, tears filling my eyes. My thoughts raced, torn between truth and the consequences. I didn't answer her question, so she asked me again.

"Why are you protecting the person who tried to kill you? Is it because it's the man you love? Ethan Hall."

How could I tell her? How could I break Ethan's heart like this? But the detective's relentless gaze broke through my resistance, and my resolve crumbled.

"It wasn't Ethan. It was a woman," I said.

"Christina Garza?"

I wish; it would make this nice and easy.

"It wasn't Christina," I whispered.

Galovich raised an eyebrow, prompting me to continue. And, finally, I told her what she wanted to know.

"It was Kayla. Kayla Hall. Ethan's ex-wife."

The detective sat back slightly, absorbing this revelation with a careful expression. "Why didn't you tell me immediately?"

I looked up, tears running down my cheeks now, my voice strained with emotion. "Because of Ethan. She's the mother to his only child. I didn't want to be the one to destroy that for him. I didn't want him to blame me for breaking up the family for good."

Galovich nodded, her expression softening slightly.

I turned away from her. I could only hope Ethan would someday understand. And maybe, just maybe, he'd forgive me. And finally find his way back to me. *Can't he see we belong together?* I just had to be patient.

The detective got up from the chair. She looked at me with accusatory eyes. Maybe I was just being paranoid. Cops always look at people like they're guilty of something.

"You're lucky that Kayla is a lousy shot. According to the doctor from the gunshot wound, she was very close to you when she shot you," Galovich said, as if to gauge my reaction.

"Lucky me," I said sarcastically. "What happens next?"

"We'll pick Kayla up for questioning. I'll be in touch," she said as she walked out of the room.

I sat back in the bed. I couldn't help but smile broadly.

THIRTY-SEVEN
DETECTIVE NORA GALOVICH

I stood behind the two-way mirror, arms crossed, my gaze fixed on Kayla, who sat alone in the interrogation room. They intentionally made the room cramped and cold, and the chair stiff and uncomfortable; these were psychological tactics meant to unsettle even the most composed criminals.

Kayla was shivering, pulling her jacket tightly around herself, her eyes wide and uncertain as she scanned the room's bare walls. Letting suspects sit alone in that room for a while was also an interrogation tactic.

Beside me stood my boss, Lieutenant Evan Lee, and another major crime Detective Bill Martinez, both watching Kayla through the glass as well. The only sound was the faint hum of the air conditioning and the occasional shuffling of Kayla's feet on the cold linoleum floor coming through the intercom.

"What do you think?" Lee asked, breaking the heavy silence.

I studied Kayla. She was visibly nervous—understandable for someone who had never set foot in an interrogation room before. Her hands trembled slightly as she fidgeted with the hem of her jacket.

"Honestly, sir, it doesn't track," I said. "I don't see a motive here. She's the one who initiated divorce proceedings against Ethan Hall. Why would she try to kill one of his girlfriends? Besides, Ethan and Jade are no longer in a romantic relationship."

Lee and Martinez nodded slowly in unison, considering my words. Just then, Deputy Rivera entered the room, clutching his notepad.

I had been waiting for him to provide an update. "What did you find?"

Rivera glanced down briefly at his notes before looking up, eager to share his findings. "Her alibi checks out completely. A thousand percent. I mean, it's one of the most airtight alibis I've ever encountered. She was working her shift at the hospital. Multiple witnesses confirmed seeing her—doctors, nurses, even a couple of patients. Security footage puts her there, in the hospital, exactly at the time Jade Sommer was shot. Kayla Hall is absolutely not our shooter."

My interrogation had just become an interview; that didn't come as a surprise, but I felt a surge of frustration. Jade Sommer had lied straight to my face, and I was done putting up with her nonsense. "All right," I said firmly. "I'm going in. Do me a favor and bring Ethan Hall into the interview room. I want to talk to them both."

Rivera scurried off.

"That's how I would play it," Martinez said with a grin.

Stepping into the interview room, I closed the door quietly behind me. Kayla's eyes shot up in both relief and concern. She had been waiting here alone for almost an hour.

"Detective, what's going on? Is Ethan okay?" Her voice trembled slightly.

"Ethan's fine," I assured her. "He's in the waiting room. Deputy Rivera's bringing him here now."

Just then, the door opened again, and the deputy ushered Ethan inside, closing the door behind him. "What the hell is going on? Why are you interrogating Kayla? Is she under arrest?" His voice shook with anger.

I motioned for him to sit down. "Relax, Ethan. She's not under arrest. She's not even handcuffed. We just had some questions. Please, sit."

"About what?" Ethan snapped, reluctantly taking a seat next to Kayla, placing a protective hand on her shoulder. Kayla shrugged it off.

"You both know Jade Sommer was shot last night," I began.

Kayla stared at me incredulously. "Wait, you don't think that I had anything to do with that, do you?"

"No. We know for a fact you didn't shoot Jade Sommer. We checked thoroughly, and your alibi is ironclad."

The confusion lingered. "Why would you even need to check an alibi for me?"

I hesitated then spoke directly, watching for their reactions. "Because Jade Sommer told us it was you who shot her."

Ethan's eyes widened in fury, while Kayla looked genuinely dumbfounded, her mouth hanging open.

"What?" Ethan's voice rose sharply. "That's insane! Kayla would never—"

"Why would she say that?" Kayla interrupted. "I don't understand."

"Kayla, can you think of any reason—any at all—why Jade would accuse you? Is there some conflict, argument, anything recent between you two?" I asked.

Kayla shook her head, eyes brimming with tears. "No. Nothing at all. Ethan dated her. But I don't care. We're divorced. I mean, obviously we've both been caught up in all this chaos with Christina, but that's it. I've never confronted her, never even met her in person."

Ethan cupped his hands and placed them on the table, clearly distressed by her reaction. "This is ridiculous, Detective. It's obviously Christina who shot Jade. Burned down her house. And tried to run me down. She's been threatening us all for weeks. And you can't catch her, so she just keeps trying until one of us ends up dead. Yet you drag Kayla in here, accusing her..."

I raised my hand, signaling for him to calm down. "Ethan, we're not saying Kayla is responsible. We're doing our due diligence because Jade accused Kayla specifically. So now I need to figure out why she would do that. Any ideas?"

Dejected, Ethan sat back. I had knocked the wind from his sail, but Both Ethan and Kayla shook their heads and said they had no clue why Jade would finger Kayla as the shooter.

"So what happens now?" Kayla asked.

"You're free to go," I told her. "But please, stay reachable."

Ethan stood up, upset again. "Of course she'll be reachable. And maybe, Detective, it's time you stopped listening to Jade Sommer and started focusing on finding Christina once and for all."

I didn't answer, scrutinizing them as they left the room. Once alone, I allowed my mind to spin in confusion and frustration.

Why had Jade lied to me? It seemed she was trying to protect the shooter. But why? And who was the shooter?

Just then, Lee showed up at the door, holding a piece of paper in his hands with a big smile.

"What have you got there?" I asked.

"Preliminary ballistic report from the casing found at the Sommer's crime scene," he said.

I felt my heart flutter with excitement. We'd been extremely lucky to recover the single shell casing out there among the forest detritus.

"Although not official yet, the bullet seems to have been fired from a Ruger .380," Lee added. And from the smile on his face, I knew he remembered that Ethan Hall had a license for that same type of weapon.

I sat back and grinned. "What are the odds?"

"We need to get our hands on Ethan's gun, ASAP," Lee said.

"On it."

Leaving Rivera at the station to file a warrant for Ethan's gun, I made my way to Jade's house. I didn't know what sordid game these two had going with each other, but I was going to find out.

THIRTY-EIGHT
ETHAN

Upon hearing of Jade's shooting, my blood ran cold. My immediate thought was that she was dead, that Christina had finally killed one of us.

I was relieved to learn that not only had she survived, but that her wound was superficial, and she would be fine. I had been ignoring her text messages for a while now, so I felt guilty. I had to reach out to her now that she's been hurt. So, I sent her a text, brief and cautious, unsure of what else I could say. I read it. Sounded a bit cold. Like from a Hallmark card, but I hit send anyway.

Jade, I heard what happened. I hope you're okay. You're in my thoughts.

The police were frustratingly tight-lipped about the details, but I didn't need their confirmation to know Christina was behind it. Who else could it have possibly been? The cops were taking too long, chasing ghosts in the machine while Christina terrorized all of us, unchecked and unafraid. Emboldened that the police couldn't find her.

But then came the shocker. The police had picked up Kayla for questioning. I rushed down to the sheriff's department, fury propelling me through the double doors. Detective Galovich met me, her calm demeanor only fueling my outrage as she informed me that they had brought Kayla in to ask her questions about the shooting of Jade. I exploded.

"Are you out of your mind? It's Christina! Kayla would never—"

"Calm down, Ethan," Galovich said sharply, cutting through my anger. Her eyes were wide, her jaw tense. "Just wait in the lobby."

Reluctantly, I backed down. I paced the lobby, waiting for an update. Every minute felt like an eternity. Finally, a deputy came and told me Galovich wanted me in the interview room with Kayla. I would have sprinted to the room, but not knowing where it was, I had to follow the deputy as he led me down a long corridor, a bit too slowly for my taste.

He ushered me inside a room marked *Interview Room 1*. I saw Kayla and the detective sitting at a table. I was struck by how small and cold the room was, but I dashed to Kayla's side.

. . .

A COUPLE HOURS LATER, when Kayla and I finally emerged from the sheriff's department building, her face was flushed with anger and disbelief.

"One of your girlfriends sends me nasty text messages, and now the other one says I shot her?" Kayla snapped as we stepped out into the parking lot, away from the prying eyes and ears of cops. "What the fuck, Ethan?"

I opened my mouth to respond, but nothing came out. I was completely at a loss. I wanted to defend myself, to assure her none of this was my fault—but how could I say that convincingly?

Kayla shook her head in disgust. "I can't handle this drama with your love life anymore, Ethan. You understand that, right? I need space. Just—please, leave me alone for a few days."

"Kayla," I started weakly, thinking of Tyler, trying to form a protest, but her expression stopped me. Her eyes begged for peace — from me — and I knew I owed her at least that much. "Okay. I understand."

Without another word, she stormed off to her car and left. I stood alone in the parking lot, hands balled into fists. Fury surged through me again. At first I was furious at Galovich for suspecting Kayla; now that I knew why, my fury was redirected at Jade. I yanked open the car door, dropping into the driver's seat, pulling out my phone to text Jade. My fingers trembled and I couldn't type out the words, couldn't get them right. In frustration, I hit the call button. Straight to voicemail. I tried again—voicemail. A third time, voicemail.

"Jade, it's Ethan. What the hell are you up to? We need to talk. Call me back."

I threw my phone on the passenger seat. My mind went back to when I went to get my gun yesterday. I opened the gun safe, and to my shock. It was empty.

I couldn't help but think that right after my gun vanished, Jade had been shot. And I hadn't reported the theft to the police. I was planning to do that in the morning, but then I got distracted by Jade getting shot and Kayla being picked up. What would the police think when I told them my gun was stolen and I didn't report it right away. I thought about reporting the gun theft now, but how would that look to the cops?

One didn't have to be an expert investigator to know that the timing looked bad. Could Christina have stolen my gun and shot Jade? But if Christina was the shooter, why hadn't Jade said so? Why would she try to blame Kayla?

I SPENT hours at home pacing, trying to get a hold of Jade. She usually picked up right away when I called. Now she was avoiding me. If I knew the address to her place on the mountain, I would have driven there to confront her. Even if she was recovering from a gunshot wound.

As I couldn't calm down, I grabbed a beer from the

fridge and a bottle of Maker's Mark from the counter. I twisted off the cap and filled the shot glass to the brim. I drank the bourbon, then chased it with beer. It burned, a welcome distraction from the chaos. I repeated the routine—another shot, another beer. Then another.

It didn't take long for the room to spin. I collapsed in my recliner, feeling impotent, pathetic, and powerless against the madness of my life spiraling out of control. But at least I could also feel myself drifting into oblivion. So I took another shot.

I JOLTED awake to the sound of someone pounding relentlessly at my door. It was dark. How long had I been asleep? My head throbbed, my stomach heaved. The room spun. I squinted at the table beside me: four empty beer bottles, an empty shot glass, the bourbon bottle significantly drained. Disgusted and horrified by my lack of self-control, I tried to stand as the pounding grew louder, insistent, but I was too unsteady on my feet. The banging at the door would not stop. Who the hell was pounding like that?

"Hold on!" I shouted, stumbling toward the door, dizzy and disoriented. Voices muffled by the door now sounded clear, authoritative, unmistakable.

"Police! Open this door now!"

Panic pierced through my drunken haze. What was going on? Did something happen to Tyler?

I opened the door to figure out what was happening, but the cops were not here to have a conversation. Several uniformed officers, weapons trained on me, filled my narrow hallway. "What the fuck?" I said as two of them lunged and grabbed me by my arms, pulling me from the safety of my apartment into the hallway.

"Whoa, whoa, whoa, what are you doing?" I protested.

They didn't answer. They threw me against the wall across the hall and I could feel them forcibly pinning me against it.

"Ethan Hall. We have a warrant for your arrest," one officer said.

I felt the cold metal of handcuffs on my wrists as they forced my arms behind my back so roughly I thought they were going to dislocate my shoulders. I had never been arrested before. Never handcuffed. It was surreal and horrifying.

"Arrested? For what?" I said, my words slurred. I wasn't sure if that was from being drunk or because the side of my face was being squished into the wall by one of the police officers.

No one answered my question; instead, someone yanked me from the wall.

An officer got in my face. "You're not going to give us any trouble getting into my patrol car, are you, Ethan?"

"No," I said, confused.

"Good," he said as two officers, one on each side of me, held me by my arms and marched me down the hallway.

Some of my neighbors were holding their doors open, peering at me as the cops forced me into a perp walk down the hallway and down the stairwell and into the parking lot, where they shoved me into the back of a waiting patrol car. I had asked several times what this was all about, but they ignored me.

Another officer put a seat belt across my chest. I couldn't believe how cramped it was in the back of the police car. I was six feet tall. My knees pressed against the plastic that protected the front of the car from the arrestees in the backseat. The handcuffs were so tight that my arms had become numb. I sat there alone for a while, tears welling in my eyes. I felt the urge to vomit and begged for help.

"Please, I'm going to be sick," I cried out, but they ignored me. Then it happened. I threw up all over myself and onto the partition in front of me. I could taste the beer and bourbon coming up again. It was disgusting and humiliating. I couldn't even wipe my mouth or try to clean up with my hands and arms firmly behind me.

The door opened, and a welcome cool breeze from outside swept over my face.

Seeing the condition of his car, an officer cursed, "Son of a bitch!"

He slammed the door shut. I'd tried to warn them,

but they didn't listen. A few minutes later, the same officer got behind the wheel. He berated me for stinking up his car before driving away. I tried to ask him questions, but he ignored me. I felt claustrophobic and my arms hurt. I could smell the stench of my vomit.

My mind drifted back to Kayla and Tyler. I was just glad they couldn't see me like this.

THIRTY-NINE
KAYLA

As I drove to my sister's house to pick up Tyler, I tried to process everything that had been going on. For the life of me, I couldn't understand why Jade would tell the cops I shot her?

I racked my brian. Did she want to see me locked up in jail? That's something that nutjob Christina would do. But Jade?

I couldn't understand why these women in Ethan's life dragged me into their fucked up love triangle. I'm the ex-wife. I divorced Ethan. Yet there I was in the middle of this sordid mess.

I guess it was obvious why she would do that. She wanted Ethan and saw me as a threat, so what better way to get me out of the picture than sending me to prison for years? No one in their right mind would do something that horrendous to another person. It seemed to me that Jade was just as messed up in the head as Christina.

Maybe they were in on it together. Getting revenge on Ethan for dating both. *Great choice in women, Ethan.*

It's why I told him I needed space from him. I just couldn't deal with any of this shit going on in his life anymore. We were divorced, after all. I know I hurt him by saying that earlier, but frankly I didn't care. Once this was over, he could see our son, but we were through. He should just move back to L.A.

I parked in my sister's driveway. I didn't even make it to the door when she opened it with a look of concern on her face..

"What's going, Kayla?"

"I don't want to talk about this now. Especially in front of Tyler. I just want to go home. We'll talk later, okay?" She wasn't happy, but she agreed.

Back home, we settled in for the day. Tyler was playing a video game. I forced myself to keep it together for him. He didn't need to know that the police had dragged me in for questioning, nor that one of Ethan's lovers had implicated me in a violent crime. I was glad I had the day off. We did some yard work. Then I made dinner. We sat at the table, quietly eating *carne asada* tacos—Tyler's favorite—but I could barely stomach them. My mind churned relentlessly, replaying the shocked look on Ethan's face, the hurt and disbelief in his eyes when we'd walked out of the sheriff's department, and I told him I didn't want to see him for a while.

"Is Dad coming over for tacos?" Tyler asked, pulling me out of my spiraling thoughts.

"Not tonight, honey," I said, forcing a casual tone. "He's got some work stuff keeping him busy for a few days."

Tyler shrugged, seemingly satisfied with my vague answer, and returned to his tacos. We finished dinner mostly in silence, and afterward we settled on the couch to watch a superhero movie Tyler had been begging to see. But my thoughts refused to settle, swirling anxiously with each passing scene flashing on the television.

Instead of the movie, I saw images of the living nightmare that I had been dragged into flash through my mind. I went to bed early, feeling exhausted.

My ringing phone woke me up at seven thirty in the morning. I'd slept a solid few hours, which surprised me. I figured I would toss and turn in bed all night. Who would call this early?

I picked up the phone and stared at the caller ID—Detective Galovich. My heart sank. Had Jade accused me of something else? Had there been another incident? My mind raced through a thousand worst-case scenarios before I finally took the call.

"Kayla, it's Detective Galovich. Sorry to bother you so early," she said heavily.

"What happened now?" My stomach twisted with dread.

She paused for a moment before continuing. "We arrested Ethan."

My mind blanked, trying to comprehend the words. I got out of bed. "Ethan? Arrested for what?"

Another pause, longer this time. "He's been charged with the attempted murder of Jade Sommer and the murder of Christina Garza."

The room spun around me, my legs suddenly unable to hold my weight. I sat back down on the edge of the bed, my breath hitching. "What? No. That can't be right. Ethan wouldn't—"

"I'm sorry, Kayla," she interrupted gently. "We wouldn't have done this unless we had substantial evidence. I just thought you should know before it hits the news."

My vision blurred as tears welled up, hot and stinging. Ethan, arrested for murder. It made no sense. Not Ethan, not Tyler's dad, the man I'd once loved—and in many ways still did.

"Kayla, are you okay?" Detective Galovich asked.

"I—I don't know," I whispered.

"I understand it's a shock," she said sympathetically. "Why don't you stop by my office this afternoon, anytime between noon and three pm? I'll be here. I can update you on the case in person."

"Okay."

I ended the call without another word, dropping the phone on the bed. My hands trembled. How was I supposed to tell Tyler? How could Ethan, who I'd known better than anyone my whole life, be accused of something so horrific?

FORTY

KAYLA

My sister peppered me with questions when I dropped Tyler at her place again. "What is going on, Kayla?"

I waved her off. "I'll tell you later."

"You said that yesterday!"

Thanking her for watching Tyler, I left and made my way to the sheriff's department for the second time in twenty-four hours. I must have driven past the very same building thousands of times since I was a kid. Not once had I set foot inside, and now I felt like I owed them rent.

They ushered me into Detective Galovich's office, which despite being windowless felt like a strange reprieve from the suffocating interrogation room where they'd placed me the day before. Clutter filled her office, yet it felt oddly comforting, with framed family pictures on her desk and atop an overstuffed, sagging bookshelf in the corner. There were scattered case files and a collection of coffee mugs gathering dust on the top shelf with the logos of the FBI, DEA, and the Greenwood County Sheriff's Department stamped on them. A plaque thanking her for work on some marijuana task force sat above the cups. A minute later, she walked inside, drawing my attention.

"Thank you for coming down again, Kayla," Galovich said gently as she settled into her chair behind the desk. Her voice was softer than in the interview room.

"I appreciate you meeting me here, instead of... that other room."

She gave a tight smile. "I figured you've been through enough."

The awkward silence stretched out, and I took a deep breath, steadying myself. "Detective, I don't understand any of this. Ethan arrested? Murder? Attempted murder? That's impossible. I've known him half my life. He's not capable of killing anyone."

Empathy flickered briefly in her eyes. "I understand how hard this must be for you. But unfortunately, the evidence is piling up against your husband."

"Ex-husband."

She smiled and continued. "Jade Sommers admitted that it was Ethan who shot her, not you."

I swallowed hard, my throat dry. "And you believe her? Jade Sommer accused me of shooting her yesterday. Now, suddenly, it's Ethan. She's clearly lying."

"Of course I was skeptical," Galovich admitted. "She did lie at first. But she was scared, confused, trying to protect Ethan because she's in love with him."

"And he dumped her. Twice. So she's pissed off. It's obvious Jade has her own agenda. First me, now Ethan. She's trying to destroy him."

I looked away, my stomach churning with a mix of emotions. I had told Ethan to give me space, now he was in jail. But none of this made sense.

"You must have more proof than Jade's word," I said.

"We do."

"Like what?" I asked, my heart beginning to hammer.

"We found an SD card in a box of Ethan's belongings at his apartment. It had hundreds of old photos stored on it. Most of them were harmless. But two stood out." She paused, letting the silence hang. "Two images showed parts of a deceased person's body—a hand and a leg. The leg was identifiable by a tattoo—a blue morpho butterfly on the ankle."

A cold shiver traced its way down my spine.

"We have verified through a photograph, and through her mother, that Christina Garza had that same tattoo on her ankle, leaving no doubt in my mind that it was a photograph of Christina's dead body taken by Ethan."

I shook my head. "What about the harassment she has been unleashing on all of us, especially Ethan?"

She sighed. "He had access to her phone and her laptop. We believe he sent those messages to himself after he killed her, to make it seem like she had a mental breakdown and ran off so we wouldn't look for her."

"Why burn down Jade's house? And shoot her? And what? He ran himself over with Christina's BMW?"

"It's still early in the investigation, so we have more questions than answers right now. His relationship with Jade was complicated. And we didn't have any witnesses or videos of him getting run over, nor have we been able to find the BMW and we checked video cameras all around."

"So he staged that? He staged everything? Is that what you're saying?"

"It looks that way."

"That doesn't make sense. Why would he do all that?" I asked, wiping tears from my cheeks.

Galovich hesitated briefly. "We think it all started to cover up Christina's death, make it seem like she'd left town after a bad breakup. Maybe that was his original intent to throw us off. But the harassment escalated. It seems he targeted you and Jade intentionally. He wanted to reconnect with you, and the threat brought you closer together, didn't it?"

I didn't want to believe it, but it made a twisted sense—yet I couldn't accept it. "You think Ethan orchestrated everything and even killed just to get me back?"

"Like I said, it's still early in our investigation, but it fits," Galovich said gently. "When things with Jade continued to get complicated, he decided to remove her from the equation permanently, like he did with Christina. He set fire to her house. That didn't work. So then he tried another way. He asked her to meet at the park after hours, and ballistics confirmed the bullet that grazed Jade came from Ethan's gun. He now says it was stolen, but he didn't report it until after we arrested him. We have teams searching the area now, looking for the weapon."

My hands shook uncontrollably, tears stinging my eyes. "This can't be right. Ethan wouldn't do this. Not to Jade. Not to Christina. Not to anyone. I know him."

"Kayla," Galovich said. "People change. Or maybe we never truly know them as well as we think we do. Unfortunately, I've seen this over and over in my twenty years on the job. Everyone has a snapping point."

I closed my eyes, a painful lump in my throat. How could I have missed something so dark in the man I'd loved, the father of my child? I felt betrayed—not just by Ethan, but by my heart and my judgment.

"I'm sorry," Galovich added quietly, seeing my turmoil. "I really am."

I didn't respond, lost in my own thoughts, unable to

shake the devastating doubt that was taking hold about the man I thought I knew so well.

FORTY-ONE
DETECTIVE NORA GALOVICH

We spent the next couple of days putting the final nails into Ethan's legal coffin. We had enough evidence to send him to prison for life. Usually, during this part of an investigation, I was beaming with joy. All my hard work was paying off. Closure for the victim's family. Locking up the bad guy. It was why I loved a job so fraught with despair.

So why did I feel uneasy about it? Why was I not beaming like I usually did?

My lieutenant had even told me to wrap things up in the next day or two so I could get to work on a new case. There was always a new case to work on in Greenwood County. Lieutenant Lee wanted me to turn this case over to the DA's office. It would be their job to send Ethan to prison for the rest of his life, using the evidence I had collected.

Kayla was questioning the past fifteen years of her

life with Ethan, but she continued insisting that Ethan couldn't be behind all this. The sending of nasty messages to himself. To Kayla. Even threatening Tyler. Burning Jade's house down, shooting her. He would never do that, she told me with certainty, even though I could tell from her facial expression that I had planted a seed of doubt in her head about her ex-husband. That was not something I relished doing. Even the most heinous of criminals have people who love them.

I shouldn't put too much stock in it. Although they were divorced, it was obvious they were on very good terms with each other and he was the father of her only child. So she couldn't put their intertwined, complicated history aside just like that.

Why was I feeling that uncertainty in my gut?

I was going to box everything up, but Seth had sent me an Excel spreadsheet a few days before that I hadn't looked at because everything had lined up nicely against Ethan and we'd moved fast to pick him up. Still, I had to make sure not to dismiss other leads only because it was more convenient to charge Ethan and move on to a new case without looking at every piece of evidence diligently.

I drummed my fingers against the desk as I examined the spreadsheet of IP addresses from Seth. Each threatening and harassing text message and email sent to Ethan, Jade, and Kayla was tied to a specific IP address, which is like a house address for devices to communicate with each other on the internet. That is why cyber criminals avoid using their own or public Wi-Fi and use VPNs and proxy servers to hide their actual IP address.

That address would lead law enforcement right to their front door.

The number of harassing messages sent during this case was mind-boggling. From thousands of IP addresses on this spreadsheet, Seth flagged only two for follow-up. He had actually tracked down the location of those two IP addresses. The rest were untraceable.

No matter how clever, most criminals end up making a simple mistake that leads to their downfall. It seemed Ethan had let his guard down and connected to a public Wi-Fi on two occasions without hiding it. Both times from Sebastopol, a city in Sonoma County located over 260 miles south of Fairdale. Since these were the only addresses I could actually follow up on and now I had some time, I did that.

The first one was to a Starbucks in downtown Sebastopol. I knew that would lead to a dead end since hundreds of customers connect to that public unprotected Wi-Fi every day. I could get lucky if they kept video surveillance inside the cafe for longer than thirty days. But the second one intrigued me even more. It was from a nursing home down the block from the Starbucks.

I picked up the phone and called them.

The phone rang twice. Then a warm and polite voice answered.

"Good afternoon, Willow Crest Assisted Living. This is Marlo. How can I help you?"

"I'm Detective Galovich with the Greenwood County Sheriff's Department," I said. "I'm investigating a cyber harassment case and noticed that someone used your facility's Wi-Fi to send messages tied to an ongoing investigation."

"Really? That's creepy," she said, sounding interested. I was worried that she would pawn me off to her employer's legal department, but she didn't. She seemed very interested in talking to a police officer. I imagined Marlo was a true crime fan and thrilled to be part of a real investigation.

"Do any of these names sound familiar to you? Ethan Hall?"

A short pause, then: "No, I don't believe so."

"How about Kayla Hall or Kayla De Silva?" De Silva was Kayla's maiden name.

"No, those don't ring a bell, either. Sorry."

I kept going. "How about Christina Garza or Dana Garza?"

Another pause. "No, Detective, I'm sorry. Those names don't match any residents or visitors that I'm aware of. And I've been here eight years. I know everyone," she said proudly.

I figured I'd hit a dead end. But we had more than enough to nail Ethan to the wall. I didn't need this to move forward, so I was about to thank Marlo for her help and end the call when a thought struck me.

"One more name," I said. "Jade Sommer?"

Marlo's voice brightened. "Oh yes! I know Jade. She visits here often. Her grandmother has been a resident with us for three years now."

I sat up straight. Bingo.

Jade. Not Christina. Not Ethan. Not Kayla. Jade had been the one accessing the Wi-Fi at the nursing home to harass Ethan.

I forced my voice to stay calm, professional. "How often does Jade visit?"

"Oh, at least once a month, sometimes more. She's very sweet, always checking in on her grandmother. Is Jade okay?"

"She's fine," I said smoothly. "I just need to confirm —are visitors able to use the facility's Wi-Fi?"

"Oh, sure. We have Wi-Fi guest access for visitors. It's a small place, so we don't regulate it much."

"Do you keep track when someone visits a resident?"

"Yes, they get logged in."

I told her when the threatening message, sent from the nursing home's IP address, was sent. "Did Jade Sommer visit that day?"

I heard Marla tapping on a keyboard.

"Yes, she was here on that day. What is going on?"

"I can't comment on active investigations." I told her I would be in touch. She sounded thrilled.

I thanked her, hung up, and stared at the file in front of me, my mind racing.

Jade Sommer had been one of the few people besides Ethan to claim Christina was still alive and sending messages. Yet here she was, accessing a nursing home's Wi-Fi—the same network used to send harassment messages to Ethan from Christina. And I knew from the metadata Seth pulled on the photograph of Christina's body that she was already dead at that time.

I grabbed my phone and dialed Seth Wellsey. I cut straight to the point.

"Seth, I need you to pull everything we have on Jade Sommer."

"I'm doing that on Ethan Hall, as you had requested yesterday," Seth said.

"Change of plans. One of the IP addresses you sent me from Sebastopol belongs to a nursing home where Jade Sommer's sweet old grandma lives."

"Holy shit. Okay, gotcha. I'm on it."

FORTY-TWO
JADE

Kayla should have been in jail. Not Ethan. That was the plan. With her out of the way, Ethan would eventually make his way back to me. But the cops fucked it all up.

I stormed through my living room with a wine glass clenched so tightly in my hand that my fingers ached.

It wasn't fair. I had done everything right. I had played the victim perfectly, given the police the performance of a lifetime. I told them what they needed to hear. I'd handed them Kayla on a silver platter. But that bitch had a perfect alibi from work. I messed that up by not checking and picking a night when she was home alone. But still. It wasn't fair. Why did she get to have Ethan?

I took a long sip of wine, the burn of alcohol doing nothing to soothe the fury bubbling inside me.

Kayla had her chance with Ethan. She divorced

him. She threw him away like he was nothing, and now she got to be the one he ran back to? No. That wasn't how this was supposed to go. But when that detective showed up at my door tightening the screws on my story, I had no choice. I had to pivot. And there was no way I was going away so Ethan and Kayla could ride off to their happily ever after. No. Fucking. Way.

Especially after the scathing voicemail he'd left me about me telling the cops that it was Kayla who shot me.

It was always about Kayla. *Let's see if she sticks by him in prison.* I couldn't imagine her making the trek down to San Quentin with Tyler in tow. She wouldn't do it. I would. Ethan was too stupid to see that. I was the one for him. His true soulmate.

My phone rang, snapping me from my thoughts. I recognized the number. It was from my grandmother's nursing home. My concern now was for my eighty-six-year-old grandmother. Something must have happened to her. Why else would they call me?

"Hello?"

"Jade, hey, it's Marlo from Willow Crest."

"Hey, Marlo, is everything all right with my grandmother?"

"Oh, yes, of course, I'm so sorry. Didn't mean to freak you out. Your grandmother is doing great. She's having a clear day and everything. I'm not calling about her."

If she was not calling me about my grandmother,

why was she bugging me? We'd been friendly with each other after years of my visiting Grandma, but we were not friends. Especially not close enough for her to call me at home out of the blue.

"So what's going on, then?" I knew I was being snippy, but I was in a foul mood.

Marlo hesitated. "Um, it's just, well, sorry to bug you, but I had a weird call today about you."

What the hell? "Someone called there for me?"

"Yeah. And I probably shouldn't be telling you, but I'm so curious about what's going on and I just wanted to make sure you were okay."

What was she blathering on about?

"I'm fine. Who called asking about me?"

"Well, this Detective Nora Galovich called earlier today. Do you know her?"

My stomach clenched. "Yes. I know her. She was asking about me?"

"Well, it's probably nothing to worry about," Marlo said, a little awkwardly. "But yeah, she called the office today asking about some cyberstalking thing she was working on and she asked me about this guy named Ethan Hall. And um, Kayla something. Oh, and Christina Garza. Something about messages being traced to our Wi-Fi. I dunno. And then, uh... she asked if I knew you."

My entire body went ice cold.

"What?" I whispered.

Marlo sighed. "Yeah, I don't know the details, but

she was asking if I knew you and if you had access to the Wi-Fi here, and I told her you visit your grandma all the time and sure you have access to the Wi-Fi. So what's going on? Do you know?"

This wasn't happening. Not now.

"Marlo, I—I gotta go," I blurted, and ended the call before the nosy woman could respond.

I stood there, frozen. It was happening.

The cops knew. What did that mean, though? Were they closing in? I half expected the front door to be kicked open, but nothing happened. All I could hear outside was the wind howling.

My breath came in short gasps. I had been so damn careful. But they'd traced the messages to my grandma's nursing home. They would check the dates. It wouldn't take them long to put two and two together.

How could I have been so stupid? All those VPNs, burner phones, proxies.

Yet I had slipped up; thought I was connected to the VPN but had connected to the nursing home's Wi-Fi instead. How could I have been so careless? After all the precautions I had taken.

My eyes darted around the room, my thoughts racing too fast to catch.

The fire. The texts. The hit and run. The photos.
Christina. Oh, God.

The stem of the wineglass snapped between my fingers. The red liquid splattered across the table and dripped onto the floor. I let the glass go, a small shard embedded in my hand.

I stared at the mess numbly, without even attempting to clean up.

This was it.

They were going to figure it all out.

I barely felt my body move as I grabbed my car keys. It was like entering into a void when I got myself into these stressful situations. It's as if my body is put on auto pilot by the id of my psyche taking over impulsively, illogical.

Visions of the future. Me in prison. Ethan out. He and Kayla are getting re-married. The happy family, while I rot in an orange jumpsuit.

Life always liked to take a big old shit on me. Ever since I was a child. Those horrible foster homes. It's not fair. I should be the one having the happily ever after with Ethan. Not her. She had her chance. Now it was my time.

FORTY-THREE
KAYLA

I was getting ready for bed by going through my evening beauty routine. Tomorrow I had a double shift at the hospital, and I was excited about it. I welcomed the distraction it would provide from all the craziness in my life. I would be too busy to think about Ethan, Jade, the police, and the relentless nightmare my life had become since moving back to Fairdale.

Down the hall, I paused by Tyler's room. His laptop screen glowed, illuminating his face in flickering blue and white. He had headphones on, fingers tapping idly on the keyboard, and seemed completely absorbed.

"One more hour, Ty," I said, leaning against the door frame. "Then lights off, okay?"

He barely looked up. "Sure, Mom."

Tyler was so much like Ethan—single-minded, able to shut out the world and get lost in whatever held his attention. But lately it wasn't just video games. He was retreating, withdrawing. Hiding.

I used to roll my eyes when my parents worried about me spending too much time online, back in the early days of chat rooms and chain emails. Now, standing in my son's doorway, I finally understood their fear. The digital world was a force I couldn't control, a place he escaped to, where I wasn't allowed. His realm of Discord servers and Twitch streams, where he hung out with his friends instead of hanging out with them in real life.

And the divorce; that was hard enough on children. And now this. How would everything happening with his father affect him?

I shook off the unease and headed toward my bathroom, craving the warmth of a hot bath. The house was quiet, save for Tyler's keyboard clicking and the nightly chorus of crickets outside. We'd moved here for this—peace, security. Yet I had never felt more exposed to the ugliness of the world.

The hot water ran, and I watched the steam curl in the air, the whooshing sound soothing. As I unbuttoned my blouse, letting it slide down my arms, a chill prickled the back of my neck. But it wasn't from a cool breeze or the vent. It was...a presence.

I froze.

The air behind me felt different—charged. The small hairs on my arms stood on end.

Someone was there.

"Tyler?" I called, irritation masking my unease. He knew better than to barge into my bathroom without knocking.

I turned.

The words caught in my throat.

It wasn't Tyler standing there by the doorway, blocking the only way out. It was her. She just stood there, glaring at me in an almost dissociative state. My heartbeat pounded in my ears as I took a slow step back, bare feet skimming the cold tile. My back touched the sink. I turned back to the fogged mirror. Her face was partially hidden in silhouette from where she stood, but I recognized her right away.

"Jade. What are you doing here?" I whispered.

She stepped forward into the dim glow of the overhead light. I could now see her face. And what I saw terrified me. She had a blank expression, and she stood there like she belonged.

I looked down and saw a butcher knife in her hand. The blade shimmering in the light.

I sucked in a sharp breath. "Jade—" My voice cracked. "What are you—?"

She tilted her head at me, as if confused as to why I was here in my bathroom. Her lips curled into a slow, unsettling smile.

"Why are you here?" Jade asked.

I blinked, unsure how to answer that. "It's my house."

"You... you took everything from me," she murmured.

Her voice slithered through the room like smoke, curling around me, suffocating.

I stepped back again, but the sink blocked me. I had nowhere to go. My mind scrambled for logic, for an escape. But the only way out was through the crazy person standing in front of me holding a big-ass knife. And I now realized who was behind everything, including killing Christina.

She'd killed Christina for dating Ethan. And now she was going to kill me.

"Jade, please," I said carefully, forcing my voice to stay even. "You don't want to do this."

Jade's grip tightened on the knife. The blade caught the light again, another wicked silver gleam slicing over my eyes.

The bathwater continued to run, oblivious to the horror unfolding. A moment ago, its gentle rush had felt soothing. Now it sounded ominous, like war drums beating in the distance.

Jade took another step forward.

"Ethan is mine," she whispered. "You had your chance with him. But you—you just had to be in the way."

I couldn't breathe.

"We're divorced, Jade. You can have him," I said, forcing the words out. My eyes darted between her face to the knife in her hand and to the only exit—past her, past that blade.

"Liar!" she shrieked. I flinched, almost leaping onto the bathroom counter.

Then, something worse dawned on me. Tyler.

If he heard this, if he came to check on me— oh, God.

I steadied myself. "Jade, Tyler is in his room. He's only a child. Please, just leave."

She twitched at his name, something flashing across her face—a hesitation, an old wound reopening.

"They took my kids from me." Her tone had shifted, becoming distant and broken. "They said I was an unfit mother. I can't even see them without supervision." She shook her head in disbelief, her grip tightening on the handle. "They said they were better off without me."

Her wild eyes locked on mine.

"You're an unfit mother! Not me. Your son will be better off without a two-faced whore of a mother like you. He'll be so much happier with Ethan and me."

Then, in one sharp motion, she lunged at me.

FORTY-FOUR
KAYLA

Jade lunged at me in a flash of frenzied movement that sent my heart into my throat. I realized in that split second how close I was to losing everything. My son, my life—gone, if I didn't act.

Adrenaline I didn't know I had surged through my body. From the corner of my eye, I spotted my countertop makeup mirror on the vanity—polished chrome finish, heavy metal base. I likened moving it to a barbell workout. Without hesitation, I reached for it when Jade was almost on top of me. Its weight felt reassuring in my grip. A chance at survival.

As I moved to my right to grab it, Jade brought the knife down. It nicked my arm and made me grunt in pain, but it only grazed me; the blade stabbed the countertop, not my chest. I then swung the mirror, my heart thundering, bringing the metal base down as hard as I could on Jade's temple. I heard a crack so loud it ricocheted around the bathroom.

Jade hadn't expected it. Her eyes widened, her features contorting in shock and pain as she staggered, half turning away from me. I saw the muscles in her arm tense, the knife dipping. She still had a weapon. The attack hadn't ended.

Neither had I. Before she could recover, I swung the mirror again, this time crashing the thick metal base against the top of her skull with all the strength I could muster. Fear and adrenaline fueled me, terror driving my every ounce of force. The impact was sickening, a dull and violent thud. I felt the vibration through my hands, reminding me of when I played softball and crushed a ball with an aluminum bat.

Jade went down hard, collapsing to her knees, the knife slipping from her grasp. I didn't wait to see if she'd stay down. I hit her a third time with the mirror and she fell flat on the floor, face first. My breath hitched; I dropped the mirror and bolted.

Tyler had heard the commotion and was running toward me, a look of panic on his face.

"Tyler!" I shouted, sprinting through the door into the hallway, bare feet stinging against the hardwood. The tub was overflowing; I almost slipped on the wet floor.

"Tyler! Run outside!"

"Mom?" His voice cracked, high and alarmed. "What's going...?"

"Outside! Now!" I yelled, my words colliding with each other. "Go to the neighbors, right now! Call 911!"

He stood frozen for a beat, trying to process the panic radiating from me. A heavy crash behind me made me jump—Jade's body, maybe. Or her trying to stand again.

"I'll be right behind you, I promise. Now, Tyler! Go!" I repeated.

He hesitated, eyes darting past me, searching for answers. But he did as he was told, turning around and running towards the stairs. I heard his socks skidding over the hardwood. Down the stairs. And the front door opening, footsteps pounding down the porch steps into the yard. The nearest neighbor was a quarter of a mile away, so I knew help wouldn't be arriving soon.

My chest swelled with relief at Tyler's escape, a feeling that quickly dissipated. I spun, half expecting Jade to be right behind me, the knife in her hand, her eyes lit with that manic fury. My entire body thrummed with dread, the adrenaline spiking so high my hands shook. But she wasn't moving. The nurse part of me felt compelled to rush over to help her, but I knew that was stupid. *Did I kill her?* I wasn't sure I could live with having killed a human being, even under these extreme circumstances.

The adrenaline dump had been ferocious, and I almost collapsed to the floor. But I recovered and made my way down the hall. I would let the police and paramedics deal with her. I was at the top of the stairs when I heard a rustle from the bathroom—the scrape of something against the tile. I turned back, and I froze. It was like watching the boogeyman in a horror movie come back to life.

Jade was getting up. She groaned at first, then let out a guttural scream. I turned and ran downstairs so fast that I lost my footing, and almost tumbled down the steps, but I was able to recover without taking a nasty spill that might have done the job of killing me for Jade.

Tyler had made it out the door—at least he was safe. I kept picturing him running across the yard in his socks, sprinting in the moonlight toward our nearest neighbor to safety.

I reached the bottom step, intent on following Tyler out into the night. The door was wide open. Just as I reached it, I felt a weight that slammed into me hard from behind—a brutal force propelling me forward and driving me face first into the hardwood under the door frame. I had been so close to getting out of the house.

Dazed, I tried to roll over, my mind a jumble of shock and raw fear. But the pressure didn't let up. I could feel a volley of blows to the back of my head, and I heard a ragged shriek, high-pitched and furious. It was Jade on top of me. She flipped me onto my back like I was a rag doll with a savage strength I never would have imagined she possessed. Jade straddled me, her knees pinning my hips in place, and I felt the sting of her fists now pounding my face, chest, arms and shoulders. I threw my hands up to protect my face, but she was relentless, a wild animal, screaming and spitting, her voice hoarse as she called me a whore and a slut.

Blood streamed down her forehead and face from the blows of the mirror, mixing with rivers of black mascara. The combination left her looking like a demented ghoul risen from the dead, eyes bulging, mouth twisted in snarling rage. In that moment, I swear I glimpsed at the unhinged darkness in her that ran deeper than anything I'd ever known.

Jade's eyes locked on mine. Her lips peeled back in a crazed grin as she hissed, "You thought you could beat me? You thought you could take what's mine?"

I tried to shove her off, pushing at her shoulders, but she felt like solid stone. She was shorter than me, but at that moment she might as well have been a giant. My arms trembled, drained by the sheer force of her assault.

Her fingers closed around my throat, squeezing with terrifying pressure. My lungs screamed for air. Gasping, I clawed at her wrists, my nails raking her skin, but she didn't even flinch. Spittle and blood from her wounds speckled across my face as she spewed profanities, each breath reeking of rage and mania. "You had your chance!" she kept repeating over and over.

"No—stop—" I gurgled. My vision darkened at the edges as she strangled me with her bare hands, and I felt my body weakening under her weight. I thought of Tyler, of how I promised I'd be right behind him. My heart hammered with desperate fear. I couldn't die here, like this, on my doorstep. Not while my son ran barefoot into the night searching for help. I didn't want him to see my dead body lying here.

I pried at her fingers, trying to loosen her grip. But I couldn't. My lungs burned, my eyes watered from lack of oxygen. The hardwood pressed into my spine, the cold air stinging my exposed skin. The world around me blurred, a disorienting swirl of fear and faint lights as she choked the life from me.

FORTY-FIVE
KAYLA

The thoughts that fluttered through my head as I died were almost absurd—tiny flashes of my past life, of people, my parents, sister, Ethan and Tyler, and of regrets. My failed marriage. Of all the things I'd said I wanted to do but never did. And now I wouldn't get the chance.

I'd read once that drowning was among the worst ways to die, and in that final moment, as Jade straddled me with her hands around my neck, I wondered if this was what it felt like to drown. My lungs begged for air that wouldn't come. Darkness edged my vision, pulsing with a heart that seemed to beat more and more slowly.

I knew she would not stop. I could see it in her eyes. They gleamed with a terrifying, ruthless resolve that promised she would keep squeezing until I was dead.

Is this how Christina died?

My arms felt like lead. I wanted to reach up—claw at her face, dig my fingers into the open wound on her head, do anything to make her let go. But I had nothing left. My hands fell uselessly to my sides, my strength siphoned away by terror and lack of oxygen. I could barely muster a faint leg kick.

Was she always this strong? Or had she tapped into some demonic, animalistic rage granting her inhuman power? These were the questions that drifted through my oxygen-deprived brain. I tried to think of Tyler, to conjure his face into focus. That was the last face I wanted to see, not the one of my killer.

I also knew that Ethan was innocent. That they would release him from jail and he would raise our son. That offered some comfort. At least Tyler would have his father. Our boy would be okay.

I saw flashing lights and expected death, but no bright white light appeared like I imagined. Instead, the flashing lights were red and blue.

A shriek of sirens and a thunder of multiple voices erupted outside. My mind couldn't piece together what was going on, but I recognized the urgent pitch of frantic shouting, and Jade's grip slackened just enough for me to breathe again. A jolt of air seized my lungs, and I gasped, sucking in breath after desperate breath. My chest burned, my throat was raw, but I was alive. And I could breathe.

Still dazed, I blinked away tears as Jade pulled her hands from my neck and raised them in the air. Her eyes flitted around wildly, reflecting shock and maybe a flicker of regret. Uniformed shapes rushed in through the open door, voices echoing a cacophony of commands:

"Get on the ground, now, or I will shoot you!"

Jade hesitated, her eyes darting between me and the officers. For one terrifying second, she looked ready to fight them all, like some cornered beast refusing to surrender. I feared the officers would open fire and I would be caught in the crossfire. Perhaps Jade was thinking the same thing. Suicide by cop, and me as collateral damage.

Then, as though her last vestige of rage had blinked out, she sagged. Arms still raised, shoulders trembling, she allowed herself to be taken down. An officer tackled her off me and threw her to the floor. They pressed her arms and her wrists behind her back. Several other officers pointed their guns at her. She let out a ragged cry, hoarse and broken.

Hands grabbed me—strong, urgent hands. I convulsed with another cough, my throat throbbing painfully at every rasp. An officer kneeled beside me, his flashlight shining in my eyes, momentarily blinding me. I squinted, tears leaking from the corners.

"You okay, ma'am?" he asked as I sat up.

I tried to nod, but it came out as a shuddering jerk of my head. My face was wet with tears, my hair clinging to my cheeks and mouth, but I was too shell-shocked to do anything about it. I just sat there. My throat felt as if it had been shredded from the inside.

"Ma'am, are you okay?" he asked me again. When I opened my mouth to speak, only a weak, rasping sound escaped.

More officers streamed in, boots thudding on the hardwood. Her once-rabid eyes turned vacant, as if a switch had flipped inside her mind now that it was over. The blood from her scalp wound matted her hair.

Two officers gingerly helped me to my feet, asking if I could stand. My legs wobbled as though made of rubber, and I nearly collapsed again. But they held me up. Another officer wrapped a heavy blanket around my shoulders, trying to stave off my shivering.

I glanced around the room in a daze, the swirl of lights and the press of people making everything seem surreal. Sirens still wailed outside. Over that chaotic soundtrack, I heard Tyler's frantic cry:

"Mom!"

I scanned the open doorway, blinking back tears. The silhouette of a small figure stood in the yard, the flashing red and blue dancing across his face. An officer had an arm around his shoulders, but Tyler fidgeted his head bopping around looking for me.

"I'm here," I croaked. With the officers' help, I stumbled forward, each step sending a trembling ache through my muscles. Finally, I crossed the threshold onto the porch toward my son.

Tyler broke free from the officer's grip and ran to

me, arms thrown wide. His eyes shone, terror and relief mixing in that eleven-year-old face that should never have known such fear. I hugged him close, ignoring the screaming protest in my bruised ribs. I knew at least one or two were broken, but I didn't care.

For a heartbeat, the surrounding chaos faded—Jade's whimpering, the officers yelling, the swirl of sirens. All I could feel was Tyler's warmth and the desperate thud of his heart against mine.

A paramedic rushed forward, a hand on my shoulder, trying to guide me away, but Tyler clung more tightly, burying his face in my chest. I could feel his ragged breathing, the confusion in every quiver of his body. Despite the dull ache radiating across my bruised neck and shoulders, I refused to let go.

"It's over," the paramedic murmured, though the words felt hollow in the air. "You're safe now."

Safe. The word lodged in my half-disbelieving mind. I turned my head, glimpsing Jade pinned against the floor inside, the glaring flashlight illuminating her stunned, empty stare. Blood was smeared across the hardwood, a testament to how close we'd both come to crossing the line between life and death.

I pressed my lips to Tyler's hair, letting the paramedic lead me gently toward the waiting ambulance. When the paramedic told Tyler to climb into the back of the ambulance with me, he excitedly said, "Cool," his eyes widening as excitement replaced the fear that had been there just a second ago, finally allowing me to crack a smile. But even that hurt.

FORTY-SIX
KAYLA

It wasn't how I'd planned to spend my double shift at the hospital. I was supposed to be on the clock—charting vitals, checking meds, not lying in a bed as a patient, bruised and broken. Every breath dragged across my throat like a razor. Speaking was worse—each word was a small punishment. My body throbbed with the deep, pulsing ache of trauma, all movement a grim reminder of what had happened. I'd been tackled, thrown to the ground, and pummeled until my vision blurred. Two of my ribs were cracked, but the doctors told me I was lucky.

I didn't feel lucky. I felt wrecked. But I knew they were right. My body would recover from this. Still, it was bizarre to be here as a patient instead of a nurse, especially being admitted as the victim of a violent crime. I couldn't help but feel embarrassed about the entire ordeal. But it was comforting to see the faces of my colleagues and friends; I knew they were taking care of me.

A doctor informed me that with just a little more pressure, Jade could have crushed my windpipe. I tried not to think about it too much. I wanted to focus on the fact that I was still here, that Tyler was safe, and that Jade was locked away, where she could hurt no one again. And that today I was going home.

My sister brought me a change of clothes. Although Jade had now imprinted herself negatively into the memories of my house, I was eager to leave the hospital. My sister and Tyler were sharing an oversize chair by the window and an iPad, giggling. I didn't know what was so funny, but I was happy to see him smiling and laughing after what Jade had put us through as I sat on the hospital bed signing my discharge papers.

I heard a soft knock on the door. My sister yelled out, "Come in."

My back was to it, but before I could turn to see who was there, Tyler jumped from the chair.

"Dad!"

I got up and faced him. His expression showed he wasn't sure whether he was welcome. I looked at my sister, who shrugged. Tyler jumped into his arms.

"Hey buddy," Ethan said, hugging him back.

"They sprang you loose, huh?" My sister sneered.

"Just now," he said. He looked at me. "Detective

Galovich told me you were still here, so I came straight over. I hope that's okay."

When I'd first noticed him standing there, I was taken aback. However, seeing him with Tyler and his worry about what we had all gone through made me realize I was happy he had come. None of this was his fault. A lonely, divorced guy in a new town joined a dating app and went on a few dates. Probably happened every second of the day, and they don't end up going through something as horrid as what Jade unleashed on us. And on poor Christine, who'd lost her life. Ethan had to live with the guilt of knowing that, had he never met her, she would still be alive. I would not be bitter or upset. I was lucky, all things considered.

"We can talk later. I'll get out of your hair," Ethan said after I didn't respond right away.

"No. It's fine. I was just lost in thought. I'm glad you came," I said, offering a thin smile.

My sister grabbed Tyler's hand. "Hey, let's give your mom and dad a moment alone to catch up. I saw a vending machine out there. Let's go see what sugary snacks I can give you behind your mom's back," she said, winking at me as she left the room with Tyler. "Nice to see you, Ethan," my sister said as she walked by him.

Ethan stood there, his eyes weary, his face drawn with concern. He looked thinner, as if the past few weeks dealing with Jade and everything she did had drained the life out of him.

"Hey," he said, his voice thick with emotion.

I swallowed a lump rising in my throat. "Hey," I said back. "I'm glad you're out of jail, Ethan."

He hesitated before stepping closer. "They dropped all charges."

"That's wonderful," I said.

Relief flooded through me, but a wave of guilt accompanied it. He had spent days locked in a cell, accused of crimes he'd never committed. And although at first I'd refused to believe he could be guilty, I had begun to waver and believe what the cops were telling me.

"I'm so sorry, Kayla," he whispered.

I shook my head. "Not your fault. Jade played all of us."

"They found Christina's car. Her body. All of it. It's over."

The reality of it all settled over me like a heavy weight. "It's finally over."

For a long moment, we just looked at each other. There was so much history between us, so much pain and love intertwined despite our divorce.

"Tyler's okay?" he asked, shifting the subject.

"He's shaken, but yeah. He was staying with my sister while I was here, and you were in…" I didn't even want to say it.

Ethan nodded. "I begged them to release me right

away, but it took a couple days for my case to go through the system. I'm glad your sister was here to take care of Tyler for us."

The silence stretched between us again, but it wasn't uncomfortable this time. It was just... loaded.

"I deleted the dating app," Ethan said suddenly.

I blinked at him. "What?"

He gave a small, almost sheepish smile. "I deleted it. Figured I've had enough surprises from the online dating world for a lifetime."

Despite everything, I laughed. It was barely more than a chuckle, but it felt good, mentally, to laugh, though it hurt physically.

He reached out, brushing his fingers lightly over my hand. "Kayla..."

I looked down at where our hands touched, warmth spreading through me.

"Are we going to be okay?" he asked me.

I smiled. "It's going to take some time to process everything, but we're going to be okay," I said.

EPILOGUE

Ethan

THE MASSIVE CASE FILE SAT CLOSED ON DETECTIVE Galovich's cluttered desk, marking the end of a nightmare that had almost consumed all our lives.

Sitting across from her, I felt an overwhelming sense of relief mixed with lingering disbelief. Jade Sommer was finally behind bars—convicted on charges ranging from murder and attempted murder to cyberstalking and arson. But even now, knowing the full truth, it felt surreal that someone I'd been involved with had committed such horrific acts because she had become obsessed with me.

How could anyone do such horrible things because of love? At least what she perceived to be love.

A court-appointed psychiatrist explained it wasn't

really about obsessive love. He called what Jade had limerence, which was a state of involuntary obsession with another person. I wasn't her first and I wouldn't be her last. I didn't care what the shrink called it, as long as they never released Jade from prison.

Galovich leaned back in her chair, her eyes reflecting both exhaustion and pride. "It was close, Ethan," she admitted, shaking her head slightly. "Far too close."

I was still processing the truth. Initially, Kayla and I had believed Tyler's frantic run to the neighbors that night had summoned the overwhelming police response. But Galovich explained the reality was far more calculated. When she'd discovered Jade had been sending harassing messages from a nursing home in Sebastopol—where her grandmother was a resident—she had immediately sensed trouble. Unable to find Jade at home, Galovich had dispatched patrol cars to the farmhouse, saving Kayla's life.

Shocking discoveries in Sebastopol extended beyond the nursing home's Wi-Fi. Police got a search warrant for Jade's grandmother's house—which Jade was remodeling. Under a dusty tarp in the garage, the police found Christina Garza's damaged BMW, its missing mirror and dented front end perfectly matching the damages to my Jeep and to my injuries during the hit-and-run. Even more chilling, my stolen gun—the weapon Jade had used to shoot herself, framing Kayla, then me—lay hidden in the car's glove compartment.

Inside the modest home, police uncovered an elaborate control center filled with burner phones, computers, and even a dedicated dark web server. Jade had meticulously orchestrated every attack from this room. She had hundreds of text messages and emails on queue scheduled to be sent to me through the next year. Most unsettling were the photographs plastered across the walls: me, Christina, Kayla and, horrifyingly, Tyler—all targets of Jade's deadly obsession.

Beneath the crawlspace of the house lay the darkest discovery: Christina's body. Wrapped in a tarp, buried under lime to hasten decomposition, Christina had suffered multiple stab wounds, a violent end that matched Jade's escalating rage. Forensic evidence inside the BMW confirmed Jade had attacked Christina in her own car.

Galovich pieced together the timeline. Jade had killed Christina shortly after seeing her outside my apartment on the night of our first date. Jade had already become obsessed with me and had infected all my devices with spyware that tracked my keystrokes, recorded conversations, and accessed personal data. She had planted a GPS tracker in my Jeep and had installed a GPS tracking app on my phone, which was how she always knew my whereabouts and how she knew about my first date with Christina—and why she had showed up at my apartment that night. She had also planted a tracker in Christina's car that night, when it was parked in my apartment complex.

It made me sick to my stomach. I'd had no privacy from her. She had even planted a GPS tracker in Detective Galovich's car, much to her, and the sheriff's, embarrassment. If a trained law enforcement officer couldn't find the device, then I didn't feel as bad that I'd never noticed the trackers planted on me.

Jade's arrival that evening, claiming she'd forgotten her planner, had been no coincidence. Poor Christina did not know she'd briefly locked eyes with her soon-to-be killer.

Even the disturbing texts I'd received, supposedly from Christina proposing we live together, had been a part of Jade's cruel manipulations. By the time those messages reached me, Christina was already dead, her phone firmly in Jade's grasp.

Seth Wellsey's investigation revealed even more disturbing details. Jade had a history of stalking other men, including her ex-husband, who'd desperately fought in court to protect their children from her erratic behavior. Seth discovered a chilling video on one of her servers that revealed a twisted act of narcissism. Feeling invulnerable, she had recorded herself setting fire to her own home and the photographs of Christina's ankle tattoo.

In the aftermath, I grappled intensely with guilt. Rationally, I understood that Christina's death wasn't my fault, yet the persistent thought lingered: Had I never swiped right on her profile, Christina might still be alive. Dana, Christina's mother, had offered me unexpected comfort at the memorial service. Embracing me, she assured me that her daughter had genuinely cared for me, and that restoring Christina's reputation had meant everything to her family. I appreciated her not blaming and hating me for what had happened to her only daughter.

It was shocking to learn about Jade's military background: three years in the US Army Cyber Corps, ending prematurely when an obsession with a battalion commander led to her discharge. Her cyber expertise had deceived everyone, including the investigators of Greenwood County. She never mentioned to me that she had been in the Army at all.

Despite my doubts about their abilities, Galovich and Wellsey had cracked the case, which they both called one of the most twisted they had ever worked.

Sitting there, finally free from suspicion, I knew life would never go back to what it once was. Too much had happened. Too much had been lost. I was relieved that Christina's reputation had been restored, the media finally portraying her as the kind, beautiful person and devoted mother she was. Yet the painful knowledge that she'd still be alive if our paths had never crossed would haunt me forever.

For the first time in months, I could breathe. The barrage of vile messages had finally stopped. Maybe now Kayla, Tyler, and I could begin the long journey of putting the pieces of our lives back together. Whatever the future held for Kayla and me, the three of us would always be a family.

Jade

INSIDE THE COLD, sterile walls of the California women's correctional facility, I sat alone in my cell, staring into the dimly lit corridor through the narrow plastic window embedded in the heavy steel door. The plastic was scratched and cloudy from years of wear, distorting the hallway into blurred shapes and shifting shadows.

I stared blankly, drifting in thoughts that only I could truly understand. The silence around me was oppressive, amplifying my greatest fear—being utterly and completely alone.

The faint echo of footsteps pulled me from my thoughts, and I moved closer, pressing my face against the chilly plastic window, straining to see who was coming. A corrections officer slowly came into view beneath the harsh fluorescent lights lining the hallway. He paused by my cell, keys jangling softly as he unlocked the small food hatch beneath my window. He slid in a tray, then straightened, meeting my gaze.

"How are you holding up, Sommer?" His voice was unexpectedly gentle, almost sympathetic—a shocking departure from the scornful tone I'd grown used to from the other guards. After months of being labeled a twisted monster, his kindness felt like a sudden burst of sunlight cutting through storm clouds.

I studied his face carefully, silently taking in every feature. My heart fluttered, skipped, then quickened. I couldn't believe how closely he resembled Ethan—the strong jawline shadowed by faint stubble, the same expressive, sparkling brown eyes, even the broad shoulders and solid build. My pulse surged, sparking with excitement I hadn't felt since Ethan had first smiled at me, way back when we first met.

"I'm feeling better now," I murmured softly, tilting my head slightly, allowing my gaze to linger just a bit longer than necessary. A flirtatious smile formed slowly on my lips. "Much better, actually—now that you're here."

His eyebrows lifted, just slightly, in mild surprise, hesitating long enough to confirm my words had landed exactly as I'd intended. Then he chuckled, shaking his head slightly, amused but not put off, as if he'd heard some harmless joke. Without another word, he pushed the small metal hatch shut, the sound echoing with a finality that made my heart jump. Turning, he walked away down the corridor, his footsteps echoing softly, fading slowly until silence returned.

I leaned forward, pressing my forehead firmly against the scratched, cloudy plastic window, my gaze fixed hungrily on his retreating form until he vanished completely from my view.

Yes, I thought, warmth spreading from my chest down between my thighs, igniting my thoughts with renewed purpose and fresh possibilities. I was definitely feeling better.

So much better.

ABOUT THE AUTHOR

Alan Petersen was born in Costa Rica and raised in both Costa Rica and Venezuela. He moved to Minnesota for college, where he met and married his college sweetheart. Today, they live in San Francisco, California atop one of the city's famously steep streets, with their feisty Chihuahua.

Visit him online at **www.AlanPetersen.com**. You can also tune into his podcast, *Meet the Thriller Author*, where he interviews bestselling authors from the Mystery, Suspense, and Thriller genres. Notable guests include Dean Koontz, Lee Child, Freida McFadden, Walter Mosley, and many more. Discover these insightful conversations at **Thriller-Authors.com**.

Connect with Alan...

- facebook.com/alanpetersenbooks
- x.com/alanpetersen
- instagram.com/authoralanpetersen
- amazon.com/author/alanpetersen
- youtube.com/@thrillingreads

ALSO BY ALAN PETERSEN

Standalone Psychological Thrillers

The Basement

Imposter Syndrome

The Casual Date

The Elijah Shaw-Alexandra Needham Crime Thriller Series

Gringo Gulch

The Past Never Dies

Always There

Under A Crimson Moon

The Pete Maddox Thriller Series

The Asset

She's Gone

Odd Jobs

Made in United States
Cleveland, OH
01 September 2025